Edward Davies

The bishop of Africa

The life of William Taylor

Edward Davies

The bishop of Africa
The life of William Taylor

ISBN/EAN: 9783337124618

Printed in Europe, USA, Canada, Australia, Japan

Cover: Foto ©Raphael Reischuk / pixelio.de

More available books at **www.hansebooks.com**

THE BISHOP OF AFRICA;

OR THE

Life of William Taylor, D. D.

With an account of the Congo Country,
and Mission.

BY REV. E. DAVIES,

AUTHOR OF "THE GIFT OF THE HOLY GHOST," "INFIDELITY
AND CHRISTIANITY," "LIFE OF HESTER ANN
ROGERS," "THE BOY PREACHER," ETC.

"A workman that needeth not to be ashamed." PAUL.

PUBLISHED FOR THE BENEFIT OF
THE BUILDING AND TRANSIT FUND
OF WILLIAM TAYLOR'S MISSIONS,
HOLINESS BOOK CONCERN, READING, MASS.
Orders may also be sent to
ALL METHODIST BOOK STORES,

———

Price 75 cents.

INTRODUCTION.

FOR some time the blessed Holy Spirit has prompted me to write the following book, yea, it came upon me as an inspiration: so that I was compelled to write or disobey. It has seemed to me that the wonderful facts of the history of WILLIAM TAYLOR ought to be put on permanent record. For years I have been gathering material for the same. Years ago I wrote a sketch of his life. This book will give a concise and somewhat complete account of his marvellous life and extensive travels; and of his great African mission; it will also tend to provoke the zeal and self-sacrifice of others.

I write also to show how wonderfully his self-sustaining or Pauline method of support has been established; and also to show that this method by no means supersedes or disparages the work of the Missionary Society. Nay, verily! but it supplements and stimulates that work.

And, as I am not an interested party, I hope to give an unprejudiced statement of facts that will be a blessing to all.

I have gathered from all quarters a liberal amount of information concerning Central Africa, especially the region of the Congo, which is indeed a most promising mission field.

I have given a full account of Mr. Taylor's election to the office of a Bishop, and also of the facts that, in nine months after that election, he had gathered together nearly fifty missionaries, secured their passage money, and also money for a most liberal outfit; had traveled to Africa himself and held the Liberia Conference, and spent a month in that Republic in successful revival services, and greeted his colony of missionaries as they safely arrived in Africa, after their two long ocean voyages.

I write because I have the fullest confidence in the success of this God-inspired and heaven-ordained mission; notwithstanding all the objections that honest men have made against it.

I write also because, if my many friends and those of Bishop Taylor, will push the sale of this book, I hope to make it produce five hundred dollars for the Transit and Building Fund, after paying for the expense of making and selling the book.

Will the beloved of the Lord, of all denominations, help in this good work? Let us *work* here and await our *reward* in heaven.

I lay this book humbly at the feet of Jesus, earnestly praying for his benediction.

E. DAVIES.

Saints' Retreat, Reading, Mass., 1885.

CONTENTS.

THE BISHOP OF AFRICA;

OR THE

LIFE OF REV. WILLIAM TAYLOR.

CHAPTER I.

EARLY LIFE AND RELIGIOUS EXPERIENCE.

IT seems to me that William Taylor is the foremost man of God on this footstool to-day. For enterprise, hard work and *self-denial*, he shames the whole of us. It has been my unspeakable privilege to be with him at many Camp Meetings, and to converse with him on the cars and at my own home, and I am fully satisfied that since the days of St. Paul there never was another man who so completely imitated the great Apostle to the Gentiles. He claims the privilege of obeying God immediately, without conferring with flesh and blood; of hearing the Macedonian cry in the night, "Come over and help us," and of starting off immediately the next morning to obey "the heavenly

vision." His marvellous success in nearly
all parts of the world shows that he is indeed
led and sustained by the Holy Ghost. Some
one has truly said of him : —

"No man of modern times, has given greater
evidence of being divinely called to the work of
the Christian ministry, than William Taylor.
His career has been one of marvellous success,
and has resulted in the salvation of untold thousands. It matters not how irregular or eccentric
his line of operations may have been, in the
fundamental item of *soul saving*, we challange
the world to produce his equal. He has
preached to more people, traveled over a wider
portion of the earth, labored under a greater
variety of embarrassing circumstances, endured
more hardships and sacrifices, and accomplished
more, in what might be called the legitimate fruit
of ministerial toil, than any other living man.
Far beyond all evangelists known in the present
or past history of Christianity, he has pushed
his personal efforts to promote the kingdom of
God, and stands out in peerless strength and
moral grandeur, a perfect prodigy of excellence,
energy, simplicity and spirituality. The singu-
lar problem of his life and work has no solution,
except in the fact of his earnest and devout
piety. He undoubtedly has a richly endued

imagination, and possesses numerous elements of pulpit power in the highest degree. His mind is somewhat after the type of his body, robust and full of vitality, and kept under the most thorough and Scriptural control. He is genial, fraternal and deferential. There is nothing about him pretentious or assuming. No cant or special style, but everything that is grand and glorious. He blends strange extremes. We doubt if there ever lived a man with more intense domestic affections and interests. Yet he is only an occassional visitor to that dearest spot on earth, called home. He is gentle as a lamb, and yet bold as a lion. We seriously doubt if he knows how to be afraid. He seems, in the fullest sense, to have *given all to Christ.* The secret of his power, and the true cause of his success are that early in his ministerial life, he attained the blessing of entire sanctification. Ever since that event, he has been pre-eminently effective in his labors."

William Taylor was born May 2, 1821, in Rockbridge Co., Virginia. He was converted to God in early life. Listen to his own account: "The Lord Jesus took me into his arms and blessed me with pardon, when a child of about eight summers. The prophetic unction of the Holy Spirit thrilled

my heart in those days of my early boy-
hood.   My parents, though at that time
strangers to the converting grace of God,
taught me very early to read the Scriptures;
so that I got much gospel teaching in my
memory.   Hearing a colored girl repeat a
part of the experience of a colored man who
testified that he had got his sins forgiven,
and coupling that testimony for Jesus with
the Word of God, I got a basis of faith, and
was thus led to seek and receive Jesus as
my Saviour.

But, being ignorant of Satan's devices,
after some months of happy union with
Jesus, I was entangled and overcome.   One
day, when, with my little hoe I was waging
a war with the weeds in my father's cornfield, Satan came to me.   I was not acquainted with Satan then, and being invisible, I knew not his presence nor his design
upon me.   He said to my inner person:
"Have you not read what the poor sinners
did in Jerusalem when they repented and
obtained the forgiveness of their sins?"

"Yes, they sold their possessions and
goods, and parted them to all men, as every
man had need."   "Barnabas having land,

sold it, and brought the money and laid it down at the apostles' feet."

"Have you sold all your goods and given away the money?"

"No, I have not."

"Well, you see how it is, you can't be a follower of Jesus, unless you sell all you have and give the money to the poor, and moreover you never can be an owner of any property as long as you live."

I hung my head and soliloquized, "I have but little, but I must sell all and give to those who have need." I began to take stock of my effects intent on following the example of the sinners at Jerusalem. The only things I could recall, as coming under this gospel requirement, were a few calfskins, and sheep-skins, and a dogskin or two, down in my father's tan vats. I wondered how I could get them out and sell them. I wish I could, but I can't.

Satan had seized an arrow from God's quiver and thrust it through me, and stood over me in a grim, malicious self-gratification, peculiar to himself, and said "God requires you to do what you cannot do. Is it not a hard requirement?"

I said in my heart "It seems so, yes, it is so," and the pall of death was thrown over my spirit. O, if I had known anybody who knew Jesus, or could have had some Phillip near to expound to me the Scriptures, some one to even whisper in my ear, that I could understand that those principles were not mandatory, but simply historical, showing the power of Christian love, to relieve the necessities of the pilgrim Jews, who had come from all parts of the Roman world to their annual feast at Jerusalem, and whose conversion to God had changed all their plans. Many of them disinherited, and all of them detained for a time in the holy city. Without extraordinary benevolence on the part of the resident believers, to meet so great an emergency, want, and famine, and death would have come to many of their foreign brothers and sisters. A similar demand would now draw out a similar supply, for Christian sympathy and fraternal love are the same now as then. A little Scripture exposition would have saved me from that horrible defeat and a dozen years of fruitless struggles to be good, with as many failures and relapses into sin.

I had never heard of a Methodist at that time, and when I did hear of them I heard so many evil reports against them, that I wanted nothing to do with them. In course of time, happily for me, the advancing armies of the sect everywhere spoken against. covered the country in which I lived; and as far back as 1835 I joined them, but being a demoralized backslider, I was so dark and unbelieving that it was not till August 28, 1841, that I was by a miracle of mercy, restored to my standing in the family of God. I was so grateful to my heavenly Father for my deliverance from the horrible pit, and so filled with love and sympathy for perishing sinners, that, though extremely bashful and unobtrusive by nature, I commenced at once to work and witness for Jesus. God gave me success from the first day after my deliverance, so that I soon learned to test all my work for God by its effectiveness in soul-saving, and thus proved the truth of a more modern saying: "Nothing succeeds like success."

The spiritual instinct of every new-born soul exclaims

"O that the world might taste and see
The riches of his grace !

The arms of love that compassed me
Would all mankind embrace."

A few weeks after I was saved I dreamed
I was at a preaching service and at the close,
when the preacher dismissed the congregation, he remained standing in the pulpit and
sang a hymn. Most of the people in attend-
ance retired, and as I sat in front of the
pulpit looking at the minister, he suddenly
stopped his singing and fixing his eyes on
me, said, "William; God has a great work
for you to do and if you will 'confer not
with flesh and blood,' turn neither to the
right hand or the left, but follow the leading
of the Holy Spirit, your wisdom will increase
like a continual dripping into a bucket." In
my dream I saw the empty bucket and the
pure sparkling drops falling into it, and
learned from that hour never to say in res-
ponse to any call to perform duty, "Please
to excuse me, I am not prepared."

The next Sabbath after this vision, our
pastor, Rev. Wm. Enos of the Baltimore
Conference, at the close of his sermon dismissed the congregation, and while the ma-
jority of the people were retiring the preacher
remained standing in the pulpit and sang a

hymn. He stopped suddenly and looked at me, and then came down to me and said, "William you will please to go out!"

I grabbed my hat and cut for home, a distance of two miles. Striding over the hills like a race:, I was wondering what on earth I could have done that our preacher should order me out of the class meeting.

When my father returned home he said, "William, what became of you? Brother Enos sent me to call you in and I could not find you."

"No, sir; I was not to be found in those parts. When the preacher ordered me out of the house I thought it was time for me to start, and the grass had no time to grow under my feet."

"Well, you had nothing to be scared about. When you left, Brother Enos addressed the class and said, 'I have had my eye on William Taylor for some time, and I am satisfied that God has a great work for him to do, and if you think as I do in regard to him, I will be glad to give him a license to exhort.' The vote was unanimous. Then he wanted me to call you in. I was ashamed to report that you were not to be found."

I said but little, but thought much. My dream recurred to my mind with the beginning of its fulfilment, and I said to myself, "Who is sufficient for these things? I have nothing but an empty bucket, but I see how it is to be filled, and I have nothing to do but obey the orders of my Sovereign and my Saviour. He has not promised to fill me with knowledge but *with wisdom*. So that I may adapt means to ends, and with a little knowledge do great execution."

I soon began to realize the call of the Spirit, to devote my life wholly to soul-saving. Nothing else appeared to be worth living for, and I became so burdened in spirit as to jeopardize my health of body and mind.

Again the Lord instructed me in the night seasons. In my sleep an invisible person who seemed to be close to me, talked most kindly and sweetly to my spirit, reminding me of the command of Jesus, "that they should not depart from Jerusalum, but wait for the promise of the Father, what saith he, ye have heard of me." "Ye shall receive power after that the Holy Ghost is come upon you." Then continued my Heavenly

Teacher, "the prophetic spirit of Jonah shall be given unto you.

The anticipatory thrill of such a commission went through me, and I awoke, and patiently waited while I continued to work with earnestness."

Soon after he received a license to exhort, he looked at it and said, "What a responsibility and nothing to fill it but an empty bucket." That license was never renewed, for he was sent as junior preacher to Franklin Circuit in the Baltimore Conference.

God gave him souls on his first round on the Circuit, and he was reported to the preacher in charge as follows: "He is tall and slender, active and strong; wears a blue coat with brass buttons. His legs extend three or four inches lower than his pants, and he wears the broadest-toed boots that have ever been seen in these parts. He has but little experience in preaching, but he is desperately in earnest and has the stuff in him to make a preacher, and he can sing just as loud as he likes."

He travelled four circuits in the mountains of Virginia, and God gave him a harvest of souls. Then he went as junior preacher to Georgetown, D. C., and preached in the white and colored churches of that city. In the spring he opened his gospel commission in the Georgetown market, with great crowds, good order and religious interest. Then he preached in Baltimore in the churches and in the streets.

In October, 1848, Bishop Waugh appointed him a missionary to California, under the direction of the Missionary Society of the Methodist Episcopal Church.

After a five months' voyage round Cape Horn he arrived with a wife and two children in San Francisco, then a city of tents, September, 1849. For seven years in that city he "ceased not to teach and preach Jesus Christ." in the churches and in the streets, so that he was called "The Street Preacher." (See his book). So that he writes, "Having gone through a course of seven years in the Baltimore Conference and seven years in California, among representatives of nearly all nations of the earth it was manifest that I was being educated for something beyond the ordinary routine of a Methodist minister's work. I had no thought of a change, however, until, by a strange and unexpected providence, I was thrown out of the regular orbit of my itinerant life into a comet-like path leading me through immeasurable space. It was not of my choosing but was the greatest grief of my life up to that time. My ambition was to stay at home in the regular work with my wife and family; but my loyalty to God, which had been perfected during the first four years of my spiritual life, would not allow me to shrink for a moment from any responsibility the Lord might lay upon me, whether for life or death.

CHAPTER II.

WILLIAM TAYLOR AS EVANGELIST IN AFRICA.

THIS world-wide apostle of the Gentiles began his career as evangelist in 1856 under a leave of absence from the California Conference, to which he belonged from its organization. He labored in the Eastern and Western states of America and then in the Canadas. Thus he spent five years in winning souls to Christ. In 1861 he met Dr. James Brown in Canada, who had spent several years in Australia, who persuaded him to think about going to labor for Christ in that great country. After prayer and meditation he felt it to be his duty to visit the Australian colonies and assist the churches there in their great work. When he sailed for Australia his family returned to California. He spent seven months in England and Ireland, made a tour round the coast of

Asia Minor and Syria, explored Palestine,
and passing through Egypt took a steamer
at Suez for Ceylon and Melbourne, making
almost a year from New York to Melbourne.
He spent his first year in Australia in the
colonies of Victoria and Tasmania, the second year in New South Wales, Queensland
and New Zealand, and six months of the third
year in South Australia.

In New South Wales he met Dr. A. Mof-
fit of Sidney, who tried to persuade him to
visit South Africa. The Doctor had spent
six years on the coast of Africa and was well
acquainted with the missionary operations
and felt a lively interest in them.

When Mr. Taylor considered the claims
of his conference and of his family in California, and of his limited time for such work,
it seemed as though he could not go. But
the Doctor maintained that it was his firm
belief that God in his providence would send
him to Africa. " Very well," Mr. Taylor
replied, " Whenever I get an order from
Him to go to Africa, I will be off by the
first ship."

He had now been absent from his family
more than three years and he said this was

up-hill business all the time, "but since so
many men endure similar privations to catch
whales, and in the merchant marine and in
the army and naval service, I should have been
ashamed to complain, even if I had felt a com-
plaining spirit; but having the conviction that
God had appointed me a messenger to the
churches to the Southern world, confirmed by
the conversion of six thousand souls to God,
during these two years and a half, I patiently
waited the issues of Providence in regard to
my family."

In November, 1865, he received a letter
from Mrs. Taylor saying that it was un-
certain about her and the family coming to
visit him as she could not get passage on the
ship that carried the letter, this was an awful
suspense, "hope deferred made the heart
sick." The next day he travelled one hundred and twenty miles, ninety by mail coach
in the broiling sun at 110° Fahrenheit in the
shade to Wallaroo, to hold revival services.
A telegram from Sidney arrived that night
saying that Mrs. Taylor and the children had
just arrived and were all well. He had just
given up all hope of seeing them for many
months and now his wife and Morgan Stuart,

Ross and Edward, aged respectively eighteen, nine and six years, were waiting to see him, four children were already in heaven. Surprise, joy and gratitude so filled Mr. Taylor's soul that he lay awake all that night. Not long after he received the news that Morgan Stewart was thought to be dying, and he must hasten if he would see him alive. While waiting for a passage to his family he received the sad intelligence that his son had a malignant fever, so he made up his mind to get him to sea as soon as possible. At length he arrived and found his wife worn out with weary watching and the sick son too weak to see his father till morning. At day-dawn little Ross was brought to him. He asked him,

"How do you know that I am your papa?"

"My mother told me so."

He accepted his father on the faith of his mother's testimony. He then received his little Eddie, and finally embraced the "bony-wreck of his first-born, Morgan Stuart, and heard him faintly say, 'O, my father!'"

For three weary months they sat down just outside the gates of death. As he grew some better, it was decided that the best thing to

do was to take ship to the Cape of Good
Hope, arriving in time for the salubrious
winter season of Cape Colony.

This was a providential leading to visit
Africa and win souls. After a voyage of
forty-one days, they cast anchor at Table
Bay, Cape of Good Hope.

The Kaffirs in Cape Colony number 95,-
576. They were naturally a powerful race.
They are physically a fine race of people,
Their prevailing color is that of dark mahog-
any. All the chiefs hold their rank by
hereditary right. They speak a most eupho-
nious language, and every Kaffir is an ora-
tor. They are very swift on foot, and before
the mail arrangement one of them would
carry a packet of papers forty-six miles in a
single night.

Mr. Taylor's first Sabbath in Cape Town
was spent in the Wesleyan chapel, when the
Holy Spirit was manifested to many hearts.
In the evening he preached four miles away.
He was astonished at the small churches and
small congregations, compared with Australia.

During the week he found a reasonable

place for board, and began to inquire how he could spend his six months' stay.

The next Sabbath he commenced reviva: services and preached thirteen sermons in nine days; seekers were at the altar each night, and thirty the last night, but the whole machinery of the church seemed weak, twenty-nine gave evidence of conversion.

Soon his way opened to go to Port Elizabeth. He found a small church and a sleepy kind of people who wanted the meetings closed at 8 o'clock, P. M.

The first evening he dismissed the people at 8 o'clock, but they were so interested that they remained. Thirteen adults came forward as seekers, and about half of them found salvation, but the minister closed the meeting before the evangelist had time to speak to others that were weeping before the Lord. During the two weeks' meetings, from ten to twenty seekers were forward every night; many were converted. On Saturday evening he had a meeting for the Kaffirs and Fingoes, with a local preacher for an interpreter. Bnt it was hard work to speak to the people second-handed, especially when he was very weary. He preached to six

hundred people from the Court House steps
on Sunday afternoon. At the close, a man
came up and shook his hand, saying, " I
have heard you preach to the gamblers in
San Francisco, and to the sailors on Long
Wharf. I shall never forget how you re-
proved a sailor who wished the coals were in
hell that he was unloading. You told him
that was quite unnecessary, for if he was so
unhappy as to go down to that place, he
would find it hot enough and plenty of fuel."

He preached in various places in this
region and again to the Kaffirs, through an
interpreter; many were converted. Then in a
post cart, a rough conveyance on two wheels,
drawn by four horses, he was jolted over a
rough road for ninety miles, to

GRAHAM TOWN.

The houses are principally brick and stone,
and not generally over two stories high, and
the streets are shaded with lovely trees. There
is an extensive barracks for troops, both at the
east and west end of the city. May 13th
the largest Wesleyan chapel was crowded
three times with a superior class of people,

with a sprinkling of red-coats (British sol-diers) among them. Mr. Taylor preached in the morning from "But ye shall receive power after that the Holy Ghost is come upon you." He preached as usual on the personality, immediate presence and special mission of the Holy Ghost and the adjust-ments of human agents to his gracious ar-rangements essential to success. In the afternoon he preached to the children, and in the evening to seniors, and though many were convicted not one would come forward. The brethren were greatly discouraged. Brother Taylor gave them a lecture on ven-tilating their large church, so that the four-teen hundred people would not be poisoning all the air while listening to the Word of God. The house was ventilated and on Monday night about thirty were at the altar and many found peace. This good work went on for three weeks and a mighty outpouring of the Spirit was bestowed. One hundred and twenty persons, nearly all adults, gave their names as candidates for membership in the Wesleyan church. At the same time one hundred and seventy professed conversion in the meetings whose names were taken. He

says the people were very attentive, social
and affectionate.   He formed bonds of Christian friendship which will abide forever.

There was a general and wide-spread work
of God followed, so that strangers wondered.
A general in the army asked a barber who
this Mr. Taylor was who had caused such a
stir in the town.   The barber said, "Have
you not read in the Acts of the Apostles
about certain men who turned the world up-
side down?"

"Yes, I have read something about it in
the Bible."

"Well, sir," he replied, "Mr. Taylor, I
believe, is a relative of those men."

KING WILLIAM'S TOWN

was the next place of labor.   There were
about 6,000 people there, about half of whom
were Europeans, many of them English and
a number of Christian churches.   The Wesleyan chapel cost £2,000 in which the revival
services were held.   These interesting services were held on his first Sabbath, yet, with
all the skill and power of the pioneer preacher
there were no conversions that day.   And

the bar of reserve and of prejudice was not broken till Wednesday evening, when some twenty-eight young people gathered around the altar. It was indeed a moment of delicious joy as one after another of them arose and testified what Christ had done for them, till twenty of them had spoken for Christ. This was a demonstration of the Spirit that could not be gainsayed.

The Holy Ghost fell on the people on Sunday and twenty-six came forward as seekers of mercy, eight or ten of them arose and testified that they were saved. Twenty-eight adults came forward the next evening; all but eight found salvation. The work went on after Mr. Taylor left and his name became a household word in all that region. About eighty, including children, were converted in the eight days of his meeting.

Mr. Taylor longed to preach to the natives, but could make but little advance through an interpreter. But in the providence of God an interpreter was raised up who could interpret his words and make an impression on the audiences. His name was Charles Pamla, who had sold his farm and a good house that he might be a candidate for the ministry and

serve the Lord all the time.   He was six feet
high, well proportioned, quite black, regular
features and very pleasant expression, with a
sonorous voice.

The following testimony of this wonderful
native is marvellous in the Holy Ghost.   By
reading Wesley's sermons he became convicted of his need of entire sanctification.
He says, "I had a sure trust that through
the blood of Christ I would secure the blessing.   One morning very early I went to
prayer for this blessing, and while I was
praying and trusting in the blood of Christ,
I felt a small voice speaking through my
soul, saying, 'It is done, receive the blessing.'   The first thing I felt was ease from
the different kinds of thought, ease from the
world and from all the cares of the flesh.   I
felt the Spirit filling my soul, and immediately I was forced to say in my soul, 'For
me to live is Christ.'   And I gave up my
body, soul, thoughts, words, time, property,
children, and everything that belongs to me,
to the Lord, to do as he pleases."

This converted heathen began to lead souls
to Christ till he had a glorious revival, in
which many were truly converted, and many

mightily baptized with the Holy Ghost. He examined the converts carefully through one of Wesley's sermons on the Witness of the Spirit. Twenty-six members found peace that day and night, also one backslider, and nine people who were heathens promised to give up Kaffir beer and all other heathen customs, and every sin.

It is supposed that the Kaffir language is spoken by one million souls in Africa, therefore it was important to have an interpreter who could preach the gospel to them in their own tongue and who could interpret the preaching of Mr. Taylor.

A young minister heard Mr. Taylor preach a sermon on Christian Perfection, he obtained it, went home, started a revival in which hundreds were converted, was taken sick and died in a short time in holy triumph.

While Mr. Taylor was preaching to the English, Charles Pamla preached to the natives of King William's Town, with marked success. During three services nearly eighty persons were converted.

ANNSHAW

was the name of the next town where Mr. Taylor labored. There was a membership of 600 in this Wesleyan Circuit, most of them Kaffirs. Here it was that Charles Pamla became the interpreter of Mr. Taylor. So he took him alone and preached his sermon to him, filled his head and heart full of it. He had heard Mr. Taylor preach before but could not interpret it because it was in high English. So he determined to preach in low English, and asked him to stop him at any word that he did not understand. Besides, he gave him a talk on naturalness.

"But," said he, "I must speak loud sometimes."

"O yes," he replied, "as loudly as you like, at the right time. The scream of a mother, on hearing her child fall into a well, is as natural as a lullaby in the nursery. God has given us every variety of vocal power and intonation adapted to express every variety of emotion, from the softest whispers, like the mellow murmurings of the rippling rill, up to the thunder-crashing voices of the cataract." I, however, put it into "low English," so that he understood perfectly.

Their first meeting for preaching Mr. Taylor stood in the pulpit and Charles on the top step by his side. The audience room was crowded, packed even in the aisles. The Europeans were peculiarly dressed. The heathens were painted red with ochre, the men wrapped in a blanket, the women wearing a skirt of dressed leather. The text was "Ye shall receive power after that the Holy Ghost is come upon you, and ye shall be witnesses unto me both in Jerusalem and in Judea and in Samaria and unto the uttermost parts of the earth." It was entirely to believers. Charles caught and gave the ideas with great clearness. He seemed a transparent medium, through which the gospel thoughts were made luminous by the Holy Ghost. There was a profound silence all through the discourse for an hour and a quarter. There was an awful solemnity that every one seemed to feel, of the presence of a power, that, like a slumbering earthquake, would soon break fourth.

After a season of silent prayer at the close of the discourse — silent, but slightly interrupted by the uncontrollable emotions of the people — the assembly was dismissed to give time for refreshments and reflection before the evening service.

After tea, Charles in private revised the evening sermon. The text was, " As I live saith the Lord God, I have no pleasure in the death of the wicked." During the preaching of about an hour, " the beaming faces of the believers, the distorted features of the sinners, the tearful eyes of both, all in solemn silence before the Lord and the voice of his prophets, presented together a scene which neither painter nor poet can describe; and yet to be felt and witnessed, was to receive an impression never to be effaced."

An exceedingly appropriate hymn was given out and interpreted with great effect. Then about two hundred came forward crying for mercy, and soon one after another found salvation and sat quietly at the feet of Jesus, till seventy souls had professed to find peace and had given in their names. It seemed like the harmony of heaven to Mr. Taylor, and the angels rejoiced. The great evangelist felt that he could now preach effectually through a sanctified interpreter; so the spell that bound him within the lines of his native language was broken. It was a marvellous night.

The natives returned to a sunrise prayer

meeting the next morning. At 10 A. M.
there was a prayer meeting that lasted four
hours. During the three services one hundred and fifteen persons professed to obtain
salvation and gave in their names.

This work rolled on after he left till two
hundred and eighty were converted. So
that about three hundred were saved in less
than five days, which was a great marvel in
a heathen land, and through an interpreter.
It was remarkable how clearly they could
testify of their glorious experience. Besides
the local preachers were made six times as
efficient as formerly.

As these converts went singing home late
on the first evening, an old heathen heard
them and said he would go to the meeting;
so he took his two sticks and hobbled eight
miles to Annshaw, and got there time enough
for the sunrise prayer meeting and was truly
converted. But he had to give up one of his
wives, but this he did readily, retaining his
first wife and giving up his young wife and
his children.

Persecutions arose and a bitter opposition
manifested itself, a number were compelled
to keep away from the meetings, but the

work went on.   Charles Pamla went to another place and preached with so much power that eighty professed to be saved.

FORT BEAUFORT.

and the district had about thirteen thousand inhabitants, and the Wesleyans had a chapel that would hold four hundred.   This was the place where Mr. Taylor held his next meeting.   Many came from the former places of his labors to enjoy this spiritual feast.   The first service was on the Sabbath.   The house was filled with power and packed with people.   In the afternoon he preached to the children and in the evening quite a number were converted.

On Monday he preached to believers and in the evening the work went on graciously, some leading citizens were seeking God.   On Wednesday he preached on Christian Perfection with blessed results.   During these services sixty-five whites professed to find Christ.   One man when he found salvation, said, " Talk about sacrificing all for Christ! What had I to sacrifice but my sins and all my abominations? A sacrifice, indeed! Why it's a glorious riddance."

HEALD TOWN.

was the place of his next labors. The Wesleyan chapel will hold about eight hundred. The first service was to the natives, but Charles Pamla was not there to interpret; but they found a Kaffir boy, who, after private instructions from Mr. Taylor, answered a good purpose. His name was Siko. He put the sentences into Kaffir very rapidly. An extraordinary power rested upon the audience. Silence reigned, except the suppressed sobs. After the sermon the simplicity of the gospel was explained, and the way of salvation by faith, and when they were invited, about three hundred rushed forward to take the kingdom by storm. They all prayed audibly, and the floor was wet with their tears, yet none seemed to be crying louder than their neighbors. The pastor was afraid, but God was in the movement.

Fourteen whites were among the seekers. As soon as any one was converted he was placed in a seat on the side of the pulpit and had an opportunity to testify for Christ. One hundred and thirty-nine natives and seven whites gave their names as converted in one service, which lasted five hours.

In a few days after he held another service in the same place, at which God's power was manifested almost as on the Day of Pentecost. It surpassed anything Mr. Taylor ever saw. It was as the Spirit of God moving upon the waters, yea, as the Spirit that moved in the valley of dry bones and raised them up an exceeding great army.

Mr. Taylor's soul was mightily stirred as he saw this wonderful manifestation of God's power, as he thought of the millions beyond who had never heard the name of Jesus. He writes, "Oh, I felt that, dearly as I loved my country, my conference, my home, and above all my dear family, if it were the Lord's will to adjust my relations satisfactorily in regard to those sacred interests, and call me to this work, *I would hail it as a privilege to lead a band of black native evangelists through the African continent, till 'Ethiopia' would not only 'stretch out her hands,' but embrace Christ, through the power of the Holy Ghost, from the Cape of Good Hope to the Mediterranean.*"

This was a prophetic sentence, uttered in the Holy Ghost, uttered nearly thirty years before it was fulfilled, for while I am writing these lines this marvellous evangelist is leading ing a band of evangelists through the dark continent, a band of between forty and fifty men, women and children, who, with himself, have taken their lives in their hands and are willing to lay down their lives to promote the Redeemer's Kingdom among the sable sons of Ham. Instead of being a band of black evangelists they are a white band, and better than all, their hearts have been washed and made white in the blood of the Lamb.

At the second service at Heald Town there were one hundred and sixty-seven converted, making a total for two services of three hundred and six natives and ten whites saved, " By the washing of regeneration and the renewing of the Holy Ghost, shed forth abundantly upon them through Christ Jesus our Lord."

" If the stirring incidents and scenes of those two services could be recorded, they would fill a volume; but they were really indescribable." One after another would rise up and with tears and trembling, with sparkling eyes and beaming countenance, one would exclaim, " Satan is conquered ! Satan is conquered ! " An old lady lifted up her eyes and hands to God and for ten minutes at the top of her voice, exclaimed, " He is holy! He is holy! He is holy!" An old man cried out, " My Father has set me free! my Father has set me free!"

Brother Sargent, the pastor, wrote some time after, " I am happy to say that the good work still prospers at Heald Town. About sixty more have found peace since you left. More would have been saved, but I have had to be away so much." Some would plead for the pardon of their sins till daylight. "The valleys and rocks below the Mission house are literally vocal with the cries of penitents, morning, noon and night."

Mr. Temples, the native teacher, though not a poet, wrote a poem as by inspiration, about this work. I quote only a few verses:

" Equipped with the whole armor of his God,
  Prepared to fight the battles of his Lord;
His willing ' feet with gospel peace well shod,'
  And holding in his hand the Spirit's sword.

The righteous breast plate and faith's mighty shield
  Adorned his front, and turned hell's dart aside.
The law of truth which God to man revealed,
  Begirt his loins, and was his strength and guide.

With simple, earnest, supplicating prayer
  And labor hard, he made his armor shine;
Did all thy servants, Lord, such 'quipment wear,
  The fallen race of man would soon be Thine.

He saw the motley throng before him rise,
  Whose blood 'neath skins of various hues did run,
Yet souls alike redeemed with highest price
  The precious blood of God's beloved Son.

Now think awhile,' he said, ' let conscience live.
  Yourselves your judges be; then thus inquire—
Can God be just, and yet my sins forgive,
  Or must I dwell with the devouring fire?'

' The powers of darkness raged; it was their hour,
  Souls long in bondage held, and captive led,
Were struggling to be freed from Satan's power,
  Which held them bound, though Christ had bruised
    his head.

With tongue of seraphic fire. the herald cried,
  ' Believe in Christ; ' this is the record true
To save a guilty world, the Saviour died.
  He tasted death for *all* — He died for YOU !

A ray of light appeared, then Satan thron'd,
  His greatest efforts made ' To keep in peace
His house and goods ' which he so long had owned,
  But Jesus came and gave the soul release."

  Ten months after the pastor writes, that
out of about four hundred that professed conversion, not more than two or three of them

had failed to attend class meeting up to the time of my leaving Heald Town.

The old members were greatly quickened. The local preachers and class leaders were aroused to a sense of their responsibility. New leaders and local preachers were raised up. The Sabbath-school was doubled. The young people in bands would hold prayer meetings in the fields alone.

SOMERSET EAST.

On the twenty-second of June, Brother Sargent accompanied Brother Taylor to Adelaide, twenty miles on his way to Somerset, where he preached at 2.30. After the meeting he rode twenty miles further to Bedford. Mr. Edwards, the pastor at Somerset, with his cart and four, carried the evangelist the last forty miles, to his own home. Somerset is the centre of a district containing about 10,000 inhabitants. The Wesleyan chapel is small. Some came from fifty to seventy miles to attend these meetings. At each native service the chapel was crowded. Over fifty were converted in the two native services held and over twenty-five whites were saved. This world-wide evangelist was soon on the wing, and the next place of his labors was

CRADOCK.

Mr. Sargent carried him forty miles on his way, to "Dagga Boer," where he spent the night and stayed in the house of Mr. John Trollips and preached to the people. The next day he was carried forty miles further through the blinding dust. This brought him to Cradock all covered with dust, so that they had to dispose of their surplus "real estate," in the form of a very uncomfortable accumulation of dust. This place had a much larger proportion of temperance people than he had found elsewhere. It is five hundred and fifty miles from Cape Town. The mountains in this region do not rise in regular ranges, but stand out in every direction, clearly defined in a peculiarly transparent atmosphere of that region, in isolated grandeur. Huge granite mountains with many perpendicular lines, shaped like the roof and gable end of a house, yet rising to an altitude of six or seven thousand feet.

Mr. Taylor began his labors in this place by preaching to the Kaffirs at 7 A. M. through an interpreter. The blessed Spirit was there but there was no time for a prayer meeting. The same day he preached three times to the whites, and twelve professed to find peace. Here he preached to the Dutch through an interpreter, and in the prayer meeting after preaching, thirty gave their names as new converts. As opportunity afforded, the new converts were allowed to testify, and their testimonies would often lead others to seek after God.

At one time he preached to the whites and natives in a court-yard back of the mission house. The central group of the audience was composed of Kaffirs and Hottentots of every color and of every variety of native costume. They brought their sleeping-mats and spread them down to sit and kneel upon. Many of the Kaffirs neither understood the English or the Dutch, so Mr. Taylor had one interpreter speak in the Dutch, then another would interpret into Kaffir; and thus he reached all classes in one sermon. For more than an hour the gospel truths were thus dispensed in three languages at once without the break of a single blunder, or a moment's hesitation; men, women and children wept while angels rejoiced. At the close, scores of Kaffirs knelt to seek after God with cries and tears. The whites knelt in the dust and cried to God. A wonderful scene followed, and many were truly converted; so that in all the services there were over seventy whites and fifty natives that passed from death into life, and the work went steadily on afterwards; so that about three hundred of all classes were saved.

More than eighty miles from Cradock is

QUEENSTOWN,

the next field of evangelistic labor. This town is situated in the midst of a beautiful fertile region of country, with beautiful vales, extensive plains and high mountains. Many Christian friends came from other places on purpose to attend these meetings; one came one hundred and twenty miles. Some whole families were saved in these meetings which extended through five days; with three services on the Sabbath and two on the week days. The man who came one hundred and twenty miles had his two sons converted.

Pending these meetings at Queenstown, he went with a number of ministers to preach one sermon to the natives at Lesseyton and found six hundred hungry souls. But he utterly failed because his interpreter did not understand English. In utter mortification he closed the meeting, aud began to think of his absolute need of Charles Pamla to go with him and translate.

KAMASTONE.

This mission was commenced in 1847 by Mr. Shepherd. Here Mr. Taylor began meetings, July 14. The church was crowded. Many farmers had come twenty miles, besides one hundred bastard Hottentots, with a variety of Kaffirs and Fingoes. The Holy Ghost fell upon them while the word was preached. At length, the pent-up feelings and smothered emotions were so powerful that one man rushed out of the house, that he might give expression to his feelings.

In the afternoon the Spirit pierced many hearts; at the close, the whites fell down before the altar, while two hundred natives were seeking pardon. Now they gave way to their emotions mid floods of tears, sighs and groans.

These mighty meetings went on with increasing power and glory, which baffled all description. In two days and a half six sermons were preached and five prayer meetings held. The pastor baptized one hundred and sixty; many of them suffered persecution for Christ's sake.

A similar work of grace was wrought at LESSEYTON and at WARNERS and BUTTERWORTH, CLARKENBURG, MORLEY, BUNTINGVILLE, SHAWBURY, OSBORN, EMFURDISWENI and NATAL.

This marvellous, if not unequalled succession of revival services went on till, in the short space of seven months, there were supposed to be 7,937 souls converted; of these, 1,200 were colonists and the rest were Kaffirs, Fingoes and Hottentots.

These deeply interesting facts have been gathered from that blessed book, "Christian Adventures in South Africa," which I advise all true Christians to read. Many will wonder what kind of preaching could produce such marvellous effects. We remark, —

I.　He preached the *law*, as proclaimed from the burning Mount of Sinai, the law that is holy, just and good, the law that is our schoolmaster to bring us to Christ. He sought to kill before he made alive, to convict before he sought to point out Christ.

II.　He preached the *gospel* in all its wonderful and glorious provisions of *justification*, *regeneration*, *adoption* and the *witness of the Spirit*, and that no professor of religion should live without this grace.

III.　He preached *entire sanctification* to all true believers. He preached it out of the Bible and out of his own glorious experience. Indeed, he is an honest, simple-hearted, old-fashioned Methodist minister, saved from the fear of man, of death, or of devils; who dared to proclaim the whole truth, whether men would hear or forbear. Therefore, God was pleased to honor him.

IV.　His long experience in street preaching to all nationalities in California, and in nearly all the earth, gave him a great power over men to persuade them to come to Christ.

BISHOP TAYLOR IN CEYLON.

CHAPTER III.

WILLIAM TAYLOR FULFILLING HIS MISSION.

IN 1867 Wm. Taylor and his family sailed for London. He labored eleven months in England and Scotland. Then his way opened to preach on the island of Barbadoes, and then in British Guiana in South America. His family had returned to California, except his oldest son, who was studying at Lausanne. This son's sickness called his father back to Europe. In 1868, Mr. Taylor pursued his labors in the West Indies, with great success. He spent fourteen months in re-visiting Australia, where the ministers had reported a net increase of members in seven years of over twenty-one thousand.

August 6, 1870, he reached Galle, Ceylon, where God gave him one thousand converts, one-tenth of whom were fresh from Buddhism, and many from the ranks of nominal Christians.

November 20, 1870, he reached the harbor of Bombay, India. After spending a few days in the city, he started for the Northwest provinces, where the American missions were planted. After helping our missionaries in many ways for a number of months, God opened his way to establish self-supporting missions among the English-speaking people of Bombay, Madras, Calcutta and other central cities. His plan was to locate himself in a city, and stay there till souls were converted, a church was organized, a meeting house built and a missionary appointed. Observe in all these travels and labors, he paid his own expenses and supported his family from his own resources. At the same time he instructed the people to pay for their churches as soon as they were built, and meet all their running expenses, and thus his missions have kept out of debt.

About this time he began to call for volunteer missionaries from America, who were willing to come out and live among and of the people to whom they preached, independent of all missionary help, and the people pledged to sustain those that came. The first man to accept this offer was Mr. Robbins, a graduate of Asbury University, who went out to India without official appointment, and paid his own passage; who, besides toiling in the English-speaking work, learned, in the first year, to preach in the Marathi language.

These missions multiplied on every hand, and one missionary after another went out from America to take charge of them. The missionary society in some instances paid their passage-money, but no more. This whole thing was an irregularity in the Methodist church, but it was so practical, that Bishop Harris went out to India, and appointed Mr. Taylor superintendent of the South India Missions. Since then these missions have been organized into a separate conference, and they are spreading out into the " regions beyond." A number of successful camp-meetings have been held among them.

Thus a new dispensation of missionary labor has been established, which is to do much toward evangelizing the whole world. Mr. Taylor tells the converts to expect persecution, and to bear it for Christ's sake. He sends them out among their friends and their enemies to tell them what great things Christ has done for them, and they have been wonderfully successful in leading their friends to Christ.

Not being able to have men sent out fast enough, Mr. Taylor came to this country, went round to the camp-meetings, sold large quantities of his books, and sent out quite a number of men to India at his own expense.

He remarks that he was not sent out by any missionary society, and did not commence his work among the English and Eurasians in the name of any denomination of Christians. He had been laboring in foreign fields and helping missionaries of all societies of Christendom, and was glad to be honored with an opportunity of helping them to get the trains on the tracks they had laid, and to gather in the Pentecostal harvests of souls, resulting from so many years of unrequited toil.

" But when I struck the English and the Eurasian stratum of society in Bombay, I found myself outside of church organization. I at once formed our converts into ' fellowship bands ; ' self-supporting and self-acting bodies of agency for their heathen neighbors.

I knew not at the beginning what organic shape or name God would give to those New Testament churches held in the houses of our leading members."

At length these bands desired to belong to the Methodist Episcopal Church and sent in a petition to Mr. Taylor to have a regular Methodist church organized, which was done and Mr. Taylor was their pastor till reinforcements were sent on from America. Thus began the wonderful movement of

THE PRINCIPLE OF SELF-SUPPORT.

The Pauline plan of missionary work must now be considered as set forth by Mr. Taylor. He claims that in the gospel system there are three financial principles, with their appropriate methods of work.

I. *The Pioneer Principle* is that which governs men who go out at their own cost and without any guarantee of compensation.

II. *The Commercial Principle* is applicable to opened fields, proceeds on the line of estimated values, covering the law of *demand and supply*. First, In relation to labor and compensation. Second, In regard to all varieties of commercial equivalents.

Under the gospel utilization of the first principle, the pioneer ambassador for Christ pays his own expenses and preaches free of charge. Paul and Barnabas and the rest of the apostles exemplified this principle. St. Paul had no particular pleasure in making tents but he ministered to his own necessities and to those that were with him.

Dr. Coke sustained himself by his inheritance. Wesley by his authorship. Most of the pioneer work of Methodism in the Old and in the New world has been done on principle number one, by local preachers and by laymen and women.

Under principle number two "The Lord has ordained," as under the Jewish economy, so in the Christian dispensation that "They that preach the gospel shall live of the gospel."

"Under these two principles Methodism had its birth and its development in England and America to stalwart manhood before it had any Missionary Societies, and the same is true of all the branches of the church."

III. The principle number three is the *Charity Principle*.

It is that of sending the gospel prepaid, to

poor people who are not able to support the ministers sent among them. Under this principle all the asylums, almshouses, hospitals and charities of every kind are started and carried forward. All the Missionary Societies are based on this heaven-born principle. They constitute the greatest benevolent institutions in the world. Mr. Taylor claims to have the highest possible appreciation of these societies and for the missionaries that labor under them, having labored with many of these missionaries in many parts of the world.

He writes as follows: " In planting and prosecuting the self-supporting mission work to which God has called me, it is necessary to show that I am proceeding regularly under a clearly defined gospel charter, giving me the right of way among the nations, yet in no way to hinder, but in many ways to help these great benevolent missionary organizations in their work."

Mr. Taylor claims that the mission work of the world can be carried on to a great extent on the two first principles, and that those principles appeal to the better class of Romanists and heathen, and that this is a better way to reach them, and to a great extent the only way, and, therefore, the great work of converting this world *ought to be done and can be done* without going on the charity principle. That it is better for the people to pay an equivalent for the labor of the missionary than to have it free. That this principle tends to make the people more independent and self-dependent. And besides as it takes so much time to raise the money, send out and sustain the missionaries on the charity principle, that, therefore, the other principles ought to be put into the most vigorous operation, not to hinder but to help the missionary societies to convert the wicked world to Christ. Besides, the very idea that the missionary is a *charity agent*, bestowing the benefactions of other people, tends to keep the well-to-do part of the community away from them, because they do not want to be considered as objects of charity, when they are well able to pay an equivalent for all they need and would rather pay for the gospel laborers than have their labors as a gift. Hence it is a fact, as Mr. Taylor certifies, that many of the converts in heathen lands are from the poorest of the poor, while Paul's plan was first to reach the educated and influential people of the great cities of the Roman world. Mark well this point : Twelve years ago Mr. Taylor submitted to the authorities of the church the question of whether or not the gospel, under the apostolic principles and methods of self-support should have a recognition in heathen countries, and that he be allowed to build up loyal churches in those countries through indigenous or native support. Churches to take rank in paternal relationship, with all the rights and privileges of self-supporting churches at home, without the sponsorship of a Missionary Society.

At the last General Conference William Taylor brought up this question in the form of a resolution, which in substance was carried ; showing that the great legislative body of the church endorsed his methods of work. The great endorsement of his methods was in electing him a bishop.

It is wonderful how God blessed the labors of Mr. Taylor during his four years campaign in India. The General Conference of 1880 organized these missions into the South India Conference and the General Conference of 1884 made provision for the or-

ganization of a Central India Conference.   It
is also remarkable how firmly these missionaries resist all inducements to accept missionary money, and although at times they
feel their need of money, they are fully
resolved to live and die under the principle
of self-support on which they started.

Schools of various grades have been established. A paper called *The India Watchman* has a good list of subscribers. A publishing house has been organized, and books
and papers and tracts are being scattered
among the millions of India. Only omnis-
cience can see or foretell whereunto this thing
will grow. It is remarkable that so many
native ministers have been raised up who
were worthy to join the Conference, that the
natives out-number the Americans and so
they rule the Conference, and so far they
have ruled it well.

In 1882 Mr. Taylor said, " I have sent
from America to India within about six years
and a half, fifty-six missionaries. Besides
these there were fifty-seven local preachers
of Indian birth who support themselves and
yet preach almost daily. There were two
thousand and forty members, one-quarter of
them are converted natives. We pay no re_

gard to "color-lines." Fifty traveling preachers and their families are supported fron Indian resources. The pastors claims last year were about $23,943, of which about $23,694 were paid. We have twenty-seven church buildings and twelve parsonages. Brother John Baldwin of Berea, Ohio, founded the Baldwin school in Bengalore at a cost of $6,000. Mrs. Inskip is collecting funds for a girls' school at Calcutta. Rev. C. B. Ward has received $16,000 to support and develop his home for orphans. We are planted down in all the great centres of a population of two hundred and thirty-four millions."

Bishop Foster in *Zion's Herald* gives a glowing account of this marvellous development of the self-supporting principle in India. Saying these people are paying all their expenses, building good churches and excellent parsonages and supporting nearly fifty ministers. Their church property is kept nearly out of debt. They seem to glory in their work and to be ready for greater things. Every Christian will agree with me that this is a marvellous state of facts. At the same time he puts in a strong plea for giving this Conference assistance to develop more rapidly the work among the natives.

CHAPTER IV.

WILLIAM TAYLOR IN SOUTH AMERICA.

OUR hero came from India to this country to secure more laborers for South India, expecting to return and prosecute his great work in India. He found it necessary to locate, because he travelled in so many countries that he could hardly belong to any Conference; but he joined the South India Conference at its organization. Having found his men for India and sent them forward, he went home to see his family in California, —the first time in about seven years. Many wondered that he did not go to see them as soon as he reached this country, but he told me that it was the hardest trial of his life to part with his family, and also for them to part with him. It seemed as though he could not stand it; so he put it off as long as he could. Besides he was so busy in finding his men and raising the money, and sending them forward, that he had not time to visit his home till just before he left the country. Spending a short time in his *home, sweet home*, he felt that he must leave and be about his Master's work. He left his home with the fixed purpose to return to his Conference in India; indeed, the bishop in charge of that Conference requested him to return to his work; but all at once the Holy Spirit convinced him that he must go to South America and open up self-sustaining missions there.   The Spirit said to him when he started twice to go to India.

"No, William Taylor, you must not go to India now, you have established those missions there, and they are well organized. I want you to go to South America; there are millions of people there who are the next door neighbors to the United States, but Christians seem to be afraid of them because they are under Catholic sway. I want you to go down there and establish missions all along the western coast, among the English-speaking and enterprizing people who have gone down there to make money and have forgotten the God of their childhood."

"But I belong to the Methodist Episcopal Church, and the bishop says I must go back to India, notwithstanding I have told him of my call to South America."

"Tell the bishop that the Holy Ghost calls you to go and establish these missions in South America, and go and do my bidding and you shall prosper."

In obedience to this call, he left New York, for Aspinwall, as a steerage passenger, to save money, October 16, 1877. Landing at Aspinwall, he took the train across the Isthmus to Panama, a city of 15,000 people. From there he started for Guayaquil and Callao, the great seaport of Peru. Lima is an inland town of 120,000 people, the capital of Peru. Here he found eighty English-speaking Protestant families. I have neither time nor space for details, but suffice it to say that he found it impossible, at some points, to open places for missionaries, as such, but he made contracts with parties in a number of cities that they should forward the funds to pay the passage of a teacher, and subscribe so much a month for his support after he arrived.

While doing this hard work in that Catholic country, his funds ran low, so that he found it necessary, for two months, to live upon seventeen cents per day, and still he kept up his bodily vigor. At one place he could not succeed in starting a school until he had spent *a whole night in prayer.* Then the Spirit showed him that he could not do in South America as he did in India; that in some places they would take a missionary, and in others, only a teacher; but the teacher could be a Christian man, and thus he could open the way for the missionary, or become one himself in time.

One day, an ungodly man came up to Mr. Taylor and threatened to shoot him, and also the friend that was with him. Mr. Taylor seized the barrel of the gun, and they were both saved.

Having done his work in South America, he returned to the United States, and came to Boston, to the University, and without a dollar in his pocket, he began to select a dozen picked men and women to get ready to sail for South America, before a single remittance had come to hand to pay their passage.

The first draft was from his Catholic

friends in Tacna, for $436.93 for the passage of a man and wife. But, by the same mail he got a letter from Concepcion saying that it was feared that if a school should commence, it would raise a row among the people ; therefore, the money would not be sent. Then Mr. Taylor felt the need of a *Transit Fund*, to pay the passage of the missionaries and teachers, and from that time, he allowed his friends to pay for the passage of his colaborers. He hurried round and sold books, and raised money to help to fit out his men and women for South America and to secure for them furniture for their schools, and many other things. The workers went as steerage passengers, to save expense.

Rev. J. W. Collier, my friend, whom I baptized and received into the church, was one of the first missionaries to South America, also, his dear sister Edith. They both did excellent service, and both died in South America, and found a martyr's crown in the heavenly kingdom. At one time, Edith had to walk thirty miles to attend class meeting, but she was always there. They were fully consecrated, and laid down their lives for Christ.

It was wonderful how Mr. Taylor could go down among Catholic strangers and persuade them to subscribe money for the passage and support of teachers, to a man they had never seen before and may never see again. It shows the great power that God gave him, and the confidence that they had in him. He says he had the grip on them, because he paid his own expenses and worked without salary and was working for their good. And besides, he would not handle a cent of their money, but have it sent on to Phillips & Hunt, New York, to be paid out for passage money and for the support of his teachers or preachers, who were to be paid monthly.

This excellent work went on from year to year till in Nov., 1881, he had forty-three teachers or preachers in South America, besides those who had died or returned home.

THE TRANSIT FUND.

It was found necessary to establish a transit fund to pay the passage of his missionaries, and God found a man to act as treasurer in the person of Richard Grant, whose office is on Hudson street, New York city, and who has just issued a report of "Taylor Transit Fund," from July 1, 1884, to February 16, 1885, of $16,777.73 received and disbursed.

Mr. Grant is one of the grandest men on this footstool, and is wholly sanctified to God and fully devoted to the spread of the gospel to the ends of the earth. McDonald & Gill of Boston, Palmer & Hughes of New York and T. T. Tasker of Philadelphia, are agents to receive this money, and give credit respectively in *The Christian Witness*, *The Guide to Holiness* and *The Christian Standard*. These publications contain the letters from William Taylor and his missionaries. Indeed they are great helpers in this great cause ; advocating the work and defending it in every possible way.

These South American missionaries have been ordained from time to time, and one of our bishops has travelled through South America and performed the duties of his office as opportunity served.

There has been some bitter persecution there as may be expected in such an undertaking, for the Church of Rome is the same the world over, and only lacks the power to destroy Protestantism off the face of the earth. In Santiago there was a bitter assault made upon a Bible class, in which, Rev. Lucius Smith barely escaped with his life and some poor women were fearfully abused, and more than $200 worth of Bibles were burned.

But, as of old, "None of these things moved them," and the good work is rolling on in power to subdue these nine revolutionary, war-like Republics of South America, who are cursed with Spanish Catholicism, to the sway of the Lord Jesus Christ. Brother Taylor wrote a book about this time, called "Our South American Cousins," which is a live book on a living subject; read it.

It is just to say that Brother Taylor found some earnest Christian workers in South America. Padre Vaughn was a Catholic priest, a humble, hard-working man of God. Some years ago he collected funds there and had a great number of New Testaments printed and circulated. When William Taylor was in Callao 5,000 of these Testaments came to port from Baxter's London House.

William Taylor reports that in South and Central America there are eight hundred schol-

ars in his day and Sunday schools, three-
fourths of whom are of Spanish and Portuguese blood, from which we will gather the
first fruits of a harvest of gospel agency in
the near future. In our male and female
college in Chili we have about two hundred
and forty pupils; most of them of well-to-do
families. In our Santiago college there are
twelve American missionary workers. This
is a wonderful showing for so short a time.

During Brother Taylor's second visit to
South America, he felt so much the need of
a college building at Coquimbo, Chili, that
during his absence of about ten months he
was working with his own hands a part of
that time at the carpenter's bench, and was
superintending the erection of this college
building. He worked six days on the building and preached on the Sabbath, and pushed
on the work with the force of a fully sanctified body and soul. He did this that he
might have a *freehold footing* in that dark
land, and thus reduce the expenses of rent
and command a self-respect in the regions
around.

While working on this building he became
convinced of the need of a building fund and

society. So he says, " I determined to return to America and give organic shape and
legal existence to our ' Transit and Building
Fund,' so that we can buy and hold property
for our purposes." I am happy to record
that this society has been formed and such a
lund has been started, with $12,000 already
subscribed, and they purpose to build a
school in Concepcion as soon as possible.
The following letter will give an inside view
of the workings of this great mission to South
America.

WILLIAM TAYLOR'S WORK.

"The local Committee co-operating with William
Taylor in his Mission work, composed of Mr. and
Mrs. Richard Grant, Mr. and Mrs. Anderson
Fowler, and Mr. and Mrs. Asbury Lowrey, were
called together May 14, to hear letters from
Brother Taylor calling for more laborers to be
sent into South America, and to consider various
applications for employment in that territory and
in India.

After prayer and due consideration, six persons were accepted for the South American Mission, to be sent forward in May and June. It
was also resolved to send one to India, if the
transit fund shall prove sufficient, in answer to
Dr. Thoburn's appeal for more men.

William Taylor reports that the openings for self-supporting missions were never more numerous or promising than now. He finds inviting places where Christian workers of both sexes can be employed and supported, either as school-teachers, or as teachers and preachers, or as missionaries who devote their entire time to evangelistic work and soul-saving.

William Taylor's headquarters at present are at Coquimbo, Chili, from which he superintends his whole field. He is now traveling a large circuit, to relieve a sick brother, and sustains and keeps up services in a German church, preaching for them every Sabbath while he is out on the circuit. (Reader, I have perpetrated a sort of conundrum. Do you give it up? Well, William Taylor writes a sermon and leaves it to be translated and read in his absence.)

To this German organization he reads and recites the sacramental service, and administers the sacrament of the Lord's supper, in mixed English and German as best he can. This Teutonic plant has grown so fast that it is almost ready to walk about and begin aggressive work.

As indicating the hand of Providence in this movement, we have to note, that as more doors open, more self-sacrificing evangelists are offering themselves. Surely, in the light of such enlargement and devotion, our consecrated brethren and sisters will not fail to replenish the transit fund. ,

The character of the Missionaries called for are holy men and women, of sound bodies, sound minds, sound faith and sanctified hearts and lives; good education — graduates from our schools, if possible; heroes willing to work, and work for nothing, if need be; willing to suffer and not afraid to die." A. LOWREY.

Richard Grant, the Treasurer, says, " We want to make this loan and building fund $100,000, and we as the committee, have faith that it can be done."

I am happy to report that the college building at Coquimbo is free from debt and worth $10,000, and yet it drew but $1,200 from the building fund. The following is the latest news along this line :

NEW YORK, March 10, 1885.

DEAR BROTHERS MCDONALD AND GILL,—

Bishop William Taylor's work still lives. It is of God, and will never die. It affords me great pleasure to give you the names of four workers that will enter the self-supporting work of Bishop William Taylor in South America, leaving here April 1, at noon : —

Dr. A. E. Baldwin and wife, of Minnesota, go to Iquique, Peru, to take charge of school work, which will enable Rev. J. P. Gilliland, preacher-in-charge, to give all his time to the ministry. The "loan and building fund" has purchased ground for the erection of a school there, which will, we trust, be commenced this year.

Miss Laura J. Hanlon, daughter of Rev. Thomas Hanlon, D.D., principal of Pennington Seminary, Pennington, N. J., also sails, as does Miss Dixie A. Wallace, of Sturgis, Mo., sister of the wife of Rev. J. C. Horn, preacher-in-charge at Coquimbo, Chili. Miss Hanlon goes to take charge of the music department of the school that Bishop William Taylor built in Coquimbo, Chili. Miss Wallace will enter the same school as teacher.

We feel that God is giving us some of the best men and women in the church for this work. All glory to His name for His watchful care over the work! for while some would swallow it up, God seems to say, "Touch not mine anointed," and it moves on gloriously. Amen!

February 10, Prof. Willard L. Mitchell, from Baltimore, went to Santiago to take charge of the musical department of the college there. The same day Rev. John M. Baxter returned, having come home to be ordained, which took place in Centenary M. E. Church, Jersey City, March 1, by the laying on of hands of Bishop Harris. March 3, the same brother was married to Miss

Bessie Wright, my niece, who has gone with him. He has also taken with him Brother Lincoln E. Brown, from Pennington, to assist him in the above work in Callao."

RICHARD GRANT, *Treas.*

CHAPTER V.

WILLIAM TAYLOR, THE BISHOP OF AFRICA.

IT was a wonderful chain of providence that placed this world-wide evangelist in the office of a Bishop. His travels were so extensive that he had to take a location from the South India Conference, so that he could travel, and for a number of years he was a located Elder in the Methodist Episcopal Church; and as such he was classed among the laymen, and therefore was eligible to election as a lay delegate to the General Conference that met in Philadelphia, May 1, 1884. So the layman's electoral Conference of South India elected him as one of their delegates. At the time that he was elected in South India, he was working for God with all his might in South America. So the self-supporting Conference elected to General Conference the great apostle of self-support.

This election called him home, and in due time he took his seat in the General Conference. Little did he think that in twenty-two days he would be elected from a located Elder to a Bishop. He attended faithfully to his duties, and spoke but seldom, only when he had something of importance to say. The following is a part of his speech on the question of whether women should be licensed to preach and be ordained.

William Taylor said, "I stand here to speak for my friend Paul, who is not here." After speaking awhile, he said, "Now, on whom did Paul lay the legislative and administrative responsibility of the Church? Not upon the women, but upon the men, and rests his authority for so doing on God's original law found in the third chapter of Genesis. God made man and woman to go together in the same boat, and there cannot be two captains with the same authority on the same ship.

Apart from God's inherent right to rule, God did not wish to put his holy women in possession of these men in General Conference. There are plenty of men fit for this kind of work who are not fit for much else.

While the fact is, with her warm sympathies, with her heroic zeal, with her undaunted courage, the last at the Cross and the first at the Sepulchre, the woman, with her patience and love, was needed all the time at the front. He did not want her to spend her precious time in coming to General Conferences, bearing its burdens of legislation and of keeping order in the churches."

This is but a part of his speech, but will show the drift of his thoughts.

The following paper was submitted to the General Conference by William Taylor and was substantially adopted, as will be seen by reference to Report XVI. of the Committee on Missions :—

Resolved, That it is lawful and right to get people converted to God, and to organize them into self-supporting Methodist Episcopal churches in foreign countries, just as we have always been accustomed to do in the United States; and that such churches, under the jurisdiction of our Bishops, fulfilling the disciplinary conditions of membership, shall be eligible to a direct legitimate relation to the Methodist Episcopal Church, without being put under the jurisdiction of the Missionary Society; such churches opposing no bar, but assisting the Missionary Society in their work of founding missions among the poor in the same countries.

II. That the rule under which young ministers may be ordained for foreign work at the beginning, instead of the end, of their probation, may be made applicable to ministers sent to foreign self-supporting fields.

III. That the Bishops be authorized to organize the West Coast Conference of South America as soon as they shall deem it advisable.

This was a most important matter, not merely because it adopted Mr. Taylor's methods of work, but more because it fixed the policy of the church for the future. When it was proposed to fix the residence of one Bishop in India, Marshal W. Taylor moved to strike out the word "India," and put in the word "Africa," and then said : —

Mr. President, there are three reasons why we ask this. The first is a poetic one. Your fathers brought my fathers to live in America. I would get even in the matter by compelling at least one white man to live in Africa.

My next reason is a commercial one. There is a vast continent with 200,000,000 of Africans, not all of them black Africans. They are the

Barbary States, Tripoli, Morocco, and Egypt, containing many Europeans. There is West Africa, and South Africa, with its Europeans and its Americans. There is the great centre of that country teeming with millions of men and millions of women who wait for the Gospel, who wait for a general that will lead the hosts of Israel to victory. There is a country rich in minerals, abounding in precious timber, a country that, if it is brought into closer commercial relations with this country, would offer profitable employment for thousands. One hundred and fifty thousand colored men have their names now upon a petition that will come before the Congress of this nation, asking it to open a mail line of steamers between this country and Africa. A Bishop of the Methodist Episcopal Church, living in Africa, would tend, sir, in my opinion, to quicken and foster these great commercial relations which ought to exist between these great countries.

I am in haste, because I do not wish to detain you, and I proceed to give my third reason, which is an ecclesiastical reason. We have a right to supervise the work of God in Africa. We have ten Bishops now, and we will have three, four or five more for Africa, so far as visits are concerned. We want one of them to live in Africa, so that the people in Liberia and King Jimmy's Land, and Dahomy, and the people in Transvaal, and the people in Boerland, that all the people in in these countries may learn more of the great movements of this Church and more of the blessed Church in this locality.

There are men waiting for orders to move in Africa. We are told that the interests in India are superabundant, and that we have 10,000 Methodists there. We have 26,000 Methodists in Africa. We have more than 1,000 Methodists in Liberia that belong to this Church. We have a Conference that is in regular motion there. We have a work in that country that no one can do so well as the Bishops of the Methodist Episcopal Church and the missionaries of that Church.

Now, we come to you, in view of these facts, and ask you to strike out this word India, and put in the word Africa, your oldest missionary work, upon which you have poured out money and men. I imagine myself standing this morning by the grave of Miss Michener. I imagine that there are gathered around me the shades of Cookman, Burns, Cox and Roberts. I imagine that they are saying to me: " Send a Bishop, not a piece of a one, but a complete, full Bishop, to live here, to do the work of saving this dark continent for Christ."

This speech went far toward the election of a Bishop for Africa. And the following speeches by William Taylor went on in the same direction, and will be read with interest.

William Taylor of South India said :—

" Both of the Conferences of India did petition this Conference for a resident Bishop. But I may add, we do not press the petition beyond what you may consider safe and proper. We had much rather take the risk of delay than the risk of too hasty legislation on the subject. The phase that has not been touched, and that is vital to this question, is the principle of self-support in our self-supporting Conference. The principle is advocated in all the Conferences, but realized in the South India Conference from its beginning. Of course, he would have to compete with seven English Bishops in India, four of them full-fledged, and three of them Missionary Bishops. If he hopes to stand alongside of them, he must have a Bishop's palace. If not a full retinue, he must have his coach and two, fix his metropolitan city, and have his man-servant to go with him wherever he goes in all his travels, to take care of him by day and put him to bed at night. That is the custom of the country.

The cattle of Wyoming in countless millions are developed on the principle of self-support. Sometimes, when the grass is buried beneath the snow, and heavy blizzards sweep the plains, the

poor cattle have a hard time, and sometimes five
per cent. of them die in that ordeal. I said to
some of the cattle-kings out there, ' You ought
to have a little hay for such emergencies.' They
said it would not do at all ; it would demoralize
the herd. They would quit work and go for the
hay. Of course, in the cold regions of the East
you have to depend on feeding out your hay and
corn. But the multiplication of your stock is
limited by your resources in hay or corn. That
is all right. But the possibility of the unlimited
multiplication of cattle comes from the fact that
no feed is given them. They run straight along
through the years. Now there is no conflict between the two things. Do you think so? That
is the possibility we claim for self-supporting
Missions in foreign countries. Turn us out to
grass, and let ' the survival of the fittest,' go
ahead."

At another time he spoke as follows :—

William Taylor, of South India, said : " Now
Mr. Chairman, if I do not begin right at the
point do not suppose I am going to speak away
from the question. I am going to speak to it.
Now our mother across the waters is a builder
of states and nations, and furnishes them with a
full fledged organic Christianity and Resident
Bishops. Here the big daughter, fully occupied
in opening up her own great farm and in build-

ing her mansions, has only made one attempt at
founding a nation in a foreign country; also has
attempted to plant and develop in that nation the
best type of Christianity, as we believe. Now
you know the result of this wonderful attempt of
ours at nation-building and foreign church-build-
ing on the west coast of Africa, as has been so
ably stated by Brother Spencer, and the nations
are competing with each other for a foothold and
an advanced foothold in Africa. Now with our
long attempt at doing something, is it not the time
for us to do something or quit? And if to quit,
then that is equivalent to retiring from the field,
because we would not have the face to attempt
it again in a new spot. This is our oldest Mission, and our oldest Mission ought to be made a
success. I do not think you are prepared to
abandon the field, but we have reached a crisis
forcing upon us the alternative to go ahead and
do something or quit. I should regard Liberia
as a mere basis of operations. You must remember that Monrovia is a very unhealthy place. If
you send a Missionary to Africa, see to it that he
gets out of Monrovia. For, like Memphis, it is
located on the leeward of a dismal swamp. The
daily land breezes from the mountains, passing
over that swamp, charged with malaria, deal out
death to the people both in the city and in the
harbor even to the moorings of your Episcopal
ship. If the Bishop were there hard at work for

the Master six days in the week, in all working
hours, attending to the laws of health in regard
to food, sleep and Sabbath rest, he would sweat
the malaria out of him and proceed in his work,
and not die before the Lord's time."

This was not only a characteristic, but also
a *prophetic* speech. Little did he think that
he would fulfil this prophecy himself, but in
less than nine months this marvellous man of
God was holding a Conference in Liberia,
Africa, and holding revival services twice a
day and seeing from twenty to thirty souls at
the altar every time.

J. M. Buckley said: "Mr. President,
whenever Brother Taylor speaks, one poeti-
cal quotation that I learned a great many
years ago springs up:

> ' No pent-up Utica confines my powers,
> But the whole boundless Universe is—His.'

[Laughter.]

And I am happy to say that I agree with
every word that he has uttered, and would
be willing to say (if I hadn't one or two
things to mention that he has not uttered)
' ditto ' to Brother Taylor."

It is exceedingly interesting to read the

speeches of different men in the General
Conference when this question of electing
a Missionary Bishop for Africa, as recommended by the Committee of Episcopacy,
was under discussion, and after which William Taylor was elected Bishop. Some were
utterly opposed to the idea of a Missionary
Bishop, they thought one of the regular full-
fledged Bishops should go and reside in
Africa, because Bishops Roberts and Burns
were Missionary Bishops and their labors
were not very successful.

Dr. Buckley well said that Burns and Roberts were practically Missionary Bishops for
Liberia, but were not elected by the General
Conference. We ought to have a Missionary
Bishop for Africa. The idea of sending a
man to Africa for four years and then come
back, is a preposterous idea. Let us do the
best we can for Africa. A Missionary Bishop
in Africa is what? Why, he is a Superintendent of Missions with Episcopal authority.

J. W. Hamilton contended that the word
" Missionary " should be struck out, so that
there should be no restriction. "I am not in
favor, sir, of a Missionary Bishop, who is
not and cannot be a Bishop Missionary."

Daniel Ware of Liberia contended that he should be a white man, born in freedom. " Because such men have more of that pluck aud plod, that push and dare, that has always characterized the march of Methodism."

J. A. Price well said, " If we elect a Bishop he is a Bishop until he dies, or resigns, or is deposed." Who can doubt that?

The following speech was quite to the point and is full of importance : —

L. M. Vernon, of Italy, said : "Mr. Chairman, I could very heartily desire that some of the considerations which have entered into this discussion might be left aside. I do not think we can push what I call Methodism as it is, efficiently, in this way.

What is the measure that will secure the greatest efficiency for the work in Liberia, and in Africa? I am surprised at the sentiments expressed here as to the distinctions between a Bishop and a Missionary Bishop. I may be obtuse. I may not have the sentiments of honor that some of my brethren have, but I do not at all appreciate the expressions I have heard on this subject. And when I hear these expressions of Bishop and full-flegded Bishop, it seems as consistent as it would be for Mr. Stanley to de-

mand that he should be considered a full-fledged
reporter and not a reporter for Africa.

When the constitution of our Church and
Episcopacy was established, and when there was
instituted this General Superintendency, this
agency of General Superintendents that we call
the Episcopacy was created.

Is there any sober man on this floor that sup-
poses our vast plan is designed for anything less
than an Episcopacy for the whole world, as for
America? If it has been interpreted in any
other way, it is different from that of the past,
and I have never heard of a fledged or an un-
fledged Episcopacy. What we need in Africa,
is an Episcopacy for Africa. If we survey the
continent, we shall find room enough in that
broad country in which a Bishop may circle around
without feeling his limitations. I submit one or
two questions. Is not the first thought in the
establishment of this Missionary Episcopacy for
Africa — the very first idea in this work — is it
not unity in the work? We want to · use our
agencies so that from the very first step it shall
proceed upon the idea of unity. And that you
can best secure by planting a man there who has
the survey of the whole field.

The other is local security. One visit would
be useful, but two visits would be much more
useful. But it is not invidious for me to declare
that a man who is located there for four years,

and who feels the burden of the work upon his shoulders, can do more than any man who goes for a few days only, and surpervises during the day and sleeps on board the vessels during the night. We agree with Brother Taylor that we ought to enforce that work or quit the field. If we place a Bishop there he will feel that he must make the work prosper or go down with it. I have very little confidence in any Missionary work that does not go forth on that principle. We do not go forth into this field to compare with other churches simply. It is a life and death work, and it would be an imputation to say that there are not white men here who are ready to go there with the Gospel and plant it with their own blood if necessary. And if we desire to do so we can find one or two men right here who are fit for the field. I hope it will be adopted, and that we shall at least make one prompt brave effort for the salvation of Africa.

Another member of the Conference said :—

" I do not stand on color lines at all, and as for a full-fledged Bishop, the whole of us are full-fledged Bishops as regards the Scriptural order. That is the doctrine of our Church ; and as to the office, that of a Missionary Bishop is superior to that of the ordinary Bishops in proportion to the sacrifices and hazards it may involve. It is a

high responsible office for which these gentlemen
are hardly fitted. I think there is too much said
about a full-fledged Bishop for Africa. A man
who has got the grit in him and power to run this
machine won't stop to ask whether this is a Missionary Bishop or one of some other sort. His
order is that of a Presbyter in the Methodist
Episcopal Church, and his office is to lead this
grand movement, and he may be head and shoulders above ordinary fledged Bishops."

I give these quotations because there has
been such an effort made by some parties
to prove that though William Taylor was
elected and ordained a Bishop, yet he is not
a Bishop and is only a Missionary Bishop.
His name is left out of the list of Bishops in
the Discipline, and the Episcopal fund is refused for his support.

So that the man who has done and suffered
the most for the salvation of the world, and
who accepts the hardest mission field of the
world to cultivate, is left to pay his own
passage money and support himself or take
his pay from the Missionary Society, which
the General Conference knew very well that
he would not do. Having created him a
Bishop why not treat him as such? Why

not put his name in the Discipline as Bishop of Africa? Let us be calm till the next General Conference.

No discussion in the conference created more interest than this. To show the fear that some had of being elected Bishop of Africa, one delegate said that two brethren had been to him and begged him to protect them from being buried alive in such a Bishopric as that. The same delegate said to the Conference, " I know after your action last week that you do not intend to insult my white manhood with such a proposition, and the color of the blood as I feel it running in my veins this morning, would not allow me to stultify my manhood with occupying such an office if I were black."

When William Taylor's name was mentioned for Bishop he dared not to decline, but retired from the Conference to talk with Jesus about it and also that none of his remarks should by any means influence the vote. When the vote was taken he received 250 votes, 73 votes more than enough for choice, and was declared elected. This election was received with acclamation, not only in the General Conference, but in all parts of the civilized world. He was well known, and his abilities for this difficult work could not be denied. He was no stranger in Africa, as we have seen. Still it involved a self-sacrifice such as but few were willing to make. He was already sixty-three years of age; but by hard work and rigid self-denial, he had so reserved and utilized the forces of his body that he weighed two hundred and fifty pounds, without being corpulent. He has a long, flowing beard, shaggy brows and piercing eyes. "He has a wonderful endowment of physical strength and endurance, just what is needed for his peculiar work." He says that his hard work on the college building in Co-quimbo was a tonic for his system; just the exercise he needed to bring up his strength.

He was elected May 22, 1884, and ordained the next day with the other Bishops, namely: William Xavier Ninde, John Morgan Wal-den, William Francis Mallalieu and Charles Henry Fowler. He was presented for ordi-nation by Marshall W. Taylor, a man of color and Dennis W. Osborne, a Eurasian from India.

"Exactly the same form of words was used in consecrating the Missionary Bishop as in the consecration of the other Bishops, except that in the form used in connection with the laying on of hands, the officiating Bishop inserted the words, " Missionary " and " in Africa." This was done in order that the form of consecration might be in harmony with the action of the General Conference."

The next day Bishop Andrews invited Bishop Taylor to take his seat upon the platform.

Bishop Taylor responded by saying, Mr. Chairman, if you so rule, I will obey orders. I think, however, that my place is here ; but I am a loyal Methodist, and if you so order I will obey. If you should come over to Africa, then I will give you an invitation upon the platform there. [Great laughter.]

This modest and kind reply to the Bishop was very pleasing to the General Conference. The following letter speaks for itself and shows up this extraordinary man in this great emergency. It was published in *The Christian Witness:*—

242 W. LOGAN SQ., PHILADELPHIA, May 26, 1884.
REV. W. MCDONALD :—

My Dear Brother, — Your welcome l etter received. As for African Episcopacy, I never sought it, nor desired it, nor expected it to come to me; but by a sudden whirl of the wheel of Providence, it came,— the nomination, election, and ordination, all within twenty-four. hours. The presence of the Holy Spirit was so consciously manifest that hundreds of the brethren said, " This is of the Lord." I so receive it. I cannot see through it, and don't need to. I see the leading hand of Jesus, and put my hand in His to be led whithersoever it may please Him to lead me. I am sure He will not have me go back on our record in regard to self-supporting principles or work.

I have not been in India for over eight years, but have not ceased for one day in all that time to work for that land, and have sent them, meantime, over fifty missionaries. Most of my remaining years will probably be given to Africa, so far as concerns my personal presence; but I can work for India and South America as well from Africa as I have wrought for India during the past eight years of my absence, and sometime, when the Lord is pleased to give me a " summer vacation," I can visit my churches in those countries and see how they do.

Africa is the most forlorn hope of all the field before the church. The Wesleyan Missions of South Africa have the great advantages of a salubrious, healthy climate, and the support and protection of pioneer English colonies. Their

Kaffrarian mission stations were established by treaty through those colonial governments with Kaffir kings, securing the grant of lands for mission purposes, and the recognition and protection of the missionaries; and yet, with all these advantages, those faithful missionaries had from twenty to forty years of hard work to put into the grading and track-laying business, before the glory of the Lord was revealed in a Pentecostal ingathering of souls.

On the Liberian coast we have none of those advantages; and in any other part of Africa, wheresoever the Lord may lead us, we shall have to begin at the beginning of a preparatory work, like the building of a railroad to the Pacific Coast. My only hope for manifest results in my lifetime is on the principle of Mahomedan propagandism; viz., self-support on the line of the most simple, fraternal and rigid economy. All the money of all the missionary societies would be insufficient to pay the hire of the men required for such a work; whereas, the possible resources of our "Transit and Building Fund"—or, to use, perhaps, a better name, our "Foreign Educational and Church Extension Fund"—may be adequate to pay the traveling expenses of the evangelists and teachers to the country, and her itinerant tours in the country, and also for the building of houses for our various purposes; but no salaries paid at either end of the line.

Put Africa on the list of our self-supporting missions, except Liberia, which belongs to our regular Missionary Society, and whose sucklings there, possibly, cannot be weaned. It will be my pleasure to do everything I can to help the Society in her great work; but I cannot for a moment entertain the question of a let-up of any sort on the principles and mission of self-support, which God has entrusted to me as a specialty. Such a question is not debatable. No one at this General Conference has raised the question.

Let all our dear friends pray for Africa and for me, that I may clearly discern the Lord's leading, and be led by him in every movement.

There is no mandatory authority between me and the General Conference, and I am sure the General Conference will rejoice to learn at the end of each quadrennium, that the Holy Spirit is the Supreme Leader of His conquering armies in the Dark Continent.

WILLIAM TAYLOR.

The following letter will seem to show how the Bishop looked upon his election. I simply quote facts of history. There is quite a discussion going on in our church papers about Bishop Taylor. I publish the facts and the public will judge for themselves:—

A CORRECTION.

DEAR BROTHER MCDONALD:—

I see several erroneous statements in the papers in regard to the Missionary Bishop. One is, that he was elected for four years only, whereas he was elected the same as the others — for life.

Another, that he is not a Bishop of equal standing with the others. A Bishop in the M. E. Church is a Bishop — no more, no less ; the difference being that the General Conference gives to one a definite and limited Episcopal jurisdiction, whereas the other Bishops once a year fix the sphere and limits of their respective fields. Under that arrangement I would be subject to the Board of Bishops. As it is, I answer only to the General Conference quadrennially, which suits me exactly for all my varied work. The other would embarrass me.

WILLIAM TAYLOR.

He was duly elected a Bishop, with a whole continent for his diocese, and full liberty to follow his own sweet will, so long as he pleased to do right, which he always proposed to do.

The General Conference makes no reference whatever to his being an employee of the Missionary Society, and they knew very well that he never had, nor ever would accept

money from that society.   First, because he
could do without it, and Second, because he
would not be subject to their control.   The
General Conference knowing this, and making no provision for his support, must have
supposed that he would derive his support
from the Episcopal fund, if in the hurry, they
thought anything about it.   They knew that
for many years he had supported himself.
But he having taken the place of one of the
Bishops in going to Liberia to hold the regular Annual Conference, besides the other
work assigned him, to evangelize the dark
continent; and being thus cut off from the sale
of his books, on which he depended for support, his support must come from the Episcopal funds, or from his many friends all
over the world who will never see him want
for money.

Immediately after his election he wrote,
" A sudden whirl of Providence has turned
me out a Missionary Bishop for Africa.   The
honor conferred is in proportion to the self-
sacrifice and the peril involved, and the stupendous work contemplated, with the immeasurable obstructions to be encountered
in the prosecution of it."

*On the Consecration of William Taylor, Missionary
Bishop for Africa.*

Sons of Wesley come from far,
   Veterans in the holy war;
Lands of ancient high renown,
   Empires of the setting sun.
Varying shades from wide-spread zones,
   Accents strange from many tongues;
Heroes all, courageous, true,
   Gathered are for grand review.

Angels of the Church are there,
   Bishops crowned with silver hair;
Some are strong and full of cheer,
   Some with broken lance and spear
Some who long the army led,
   Now are numbered with the dead;
Shining stars of earthly lands,
   Held in Christ's Almighty hands.

Kingdom of the Christ prevails,
   Climbs the mountains, fills the vales;
Voices call from many shores,
   Multiplied are opening doors.
Joshuas new must lead the host,
   Jordans new must still be crossed;
Bring your chosen to their place,
   Pour on them anointing grace.

Towering high among them came,
   One whose soul is living flame;
Flame of zeal of living faith,—
   Flame of love that conquers death.

Angel flying o'er the earth.
   Telling of the Saviour's birth;
Telling nations, far and near,
   Christ is risen, Christ is here.

Next him stood on either hand,
   Children of the far-off lands;
Mingled blood within their veins.
   Europe's mountains, Asia's plains.
Tinge of Afric's heated strands,
   Joined with frosts of Northern lands;
Bring offering there to be,
   Bound and laid on Africa.

Son of Man to thee we pray
   Bear in mind the awful day;
When through Jew and Roman's scorn,
   Smiting hand and piercing thorn,
Bloody sweat and bursting groan,
   Treading wine-press all alone;
Fainting 'neath the accursed tree,
   Helper* came from Africa.

Son of God, to thee, we pray,
   Guard thy servant all his way;
Bear him safely o'er the deep,
   Health and strength in vigor keep.
Open up the pathless lands,
   Fire his heart and fill his hands;
Long may he apostle be,
   Toiling for dark Africa.

Latest called of nations come,
   Greet the Western rising sun;

---

* Simon, the Cyrenian

Stretch thy hands to God once more,
  Beacons blaze along thy shore.
Messengers from distant lands,
  Water now the sterile sands;
Many crowns the Christ array,
  Add the crown of Africa.

W. G. QUEAL.

CHAPTER VI.

BISHOP TAYLOR PREPARING FOR AFRICA.

BEING elected Bishop of Africa, he began to study and pray over the matter, and look around for a company of entirely consecrated men to go with him. At first he decided that no woman would be safe in that country of savages. But soon he changed his mind, and decided to take also women and children.

These devoted ones offered themselves in the spirit of sacrifice, ready to lay down their lives for Christ's sake. Several whole families offered themselves. The father in one family wrote to Bishop Taylor, "As it regards death, for me to live is Christ, to die is gain. Heaven is as near Africa as America. There is but one thing I shall have to say; we cannot be separated, we go together, for richer or poorer, in sickness and in health, till death doth us part." Who can blame them for that?

About this time Bishop Taylor issued three circulars to his friends, explaining his plans and purposes, and urging them to furnish the money for Transit Fund. He came to Boston and gave us one of his marked speeches. A good Baptist deacon stepped forward and offered to pay the passage of one missionary, which would cost $500. I refer to Deacon George M. Morse of Putnam, Conn. The Society of Friends prepared to send out two of their missionary workers, and of course paid their expenses. The money began to pour into the Transit Fund, and the Bishop started to visit his devoted family in California. From his home he sent the following letter to *The Christian Standard :—*

"REV. E. I. D. PEPPER:

*Dear Brother,—*I am again, after an absence of over two and one-half years, at home with my own heroic wife and sons. Ross my second living son, was received into the California Conference last Saturday, and elected to deacons' and elders' orders, ' under the rule,' and was ordained on Sabbath, and will stand on the list of appointments —' Missionary to Central Africa.' As I have to hold the Conference in Liberia in January and hope to found a mission in Loando, our port of entry for the interior, and as those are very, very sickly places, and as I don't wish to imperil the lives of my force for the interior by detention in those sickly regions, I will not have my main force come on till spring so as to join me in Loando in May, and proceed at once to the higher altitudes where the climate is salubrious and healthful. Over twenty heroic men and women are ready to go on short notice. The conditions are : First, That our friends in America, through our Transit Fund Society, may pay their passage outward. Second, That all our workers shall depend on God and the people they serve for daily bread. Third, That they shall receive their salary in full from our Father in heaven after their arrival in the ' heavenly Jeru salem.' I can get more workers and better workers on these terms than I can get on any other. Glory to God, the race of heroes and heroines has not run out, and never will; but a return to the Master's orders to ' go without purse or scrip ' opens a field for the manifestation and development of such. I tried for months to intimidate the holy women who wanted to go into the wilds of Africa, for I did not then think it suitable for them to go among naked savage cannibals on a line of such rigid economy and possible perils to life, but ' they wouldn't scare worth a cent.' I drew the darkest pictures possible in a letter of reply to a good minister and his wife in Michigan, offering for Africa. The minister was unmoved by any of these things and the following is the reply of his wife,—' We have just received your letter. Yes, we knew what we were writing about. We are all missionaries in this house,' (husband, wife and nine-year-old daughter). ' The only fear I have is that I am not meet to be a sharer in this grand work. It has been my heart's prayer for years, Lord, if Thou shouldst count me worthy, *send me.* I am not afraid that we shall not be supported. What are the promises? ' My God shall supply all your need.' ' Trust in the Lord, do good, dwell in the land, and verily thou shalt be fed.' Don't the Lord keep His word? Is there not plenty of land there? Well I have planted, hoed and worked potatoes, corn and other things, and can do it again. I have slept in mud huts, tents, and in the open air, with a blanket round me, the blue sky above me, with a water-dog for my pillow, and would do it again, if need be."

Mrs. Taylor came with her husband to New York when he was preparing to go to Africa. She was cheerful and happy to have such a noble husband to give for such a glorious purpose. God will share the rewards

with her in proportion to the sacrifices she
has made. She is perfectly willing to wait
for the day of the Lord.

There is another mysterious link in this
chain of providences. The very year that
this Bishop was elected, there was published
to the world the discovery of a number of
tribes who live in the heart of Africa; the
Tushalange, the Basange and the Benike.
These semi-civilized tribes live in stone
houses, with gardens around them and these
tribes have never been corrupted with rum or
Mohammedanism; they are native heathens.
These people have remained isolated from
the rest of the world, and have been spared
from the bloody invasions of hostile tribes.
Two travelers have visited them who were
the only white persons that these people ever
saw. They number no less than one hundred thousand. They live in a healthy part
of the country and are a well-to-do people
for that dark land.

Bishop Taylor's missions are to be established in the valley of the Congo river and its
tributaries. The following quotation will be
read with profit and interest, showing another
link in this remarkable providential chain :—

" The dark regions of the Dark Continent are opening to the Word whose entrance giveth light. The eyes of Christendom are turned toward Congo-land. States and empires vie with each other in the solution of the great geographical problem of the age. Diplomacy becomes the handmaid of the Church. The Congo Congress in session in imperial Berlin, in which are represented the great countries of Europe and also the United States, will shape the destiny of the hitherto unknown. Commerce and Christianity enter hand in hand for Africa's redemption.

Congo-land is the garden of Central Africa. Its salubrious climate, navigable streams, fertile soil, and the number and character of its peoples, make it a chosen field for trade and missionary effort. It stretches from three degrees north latitude to twelve degrees south of the equator, and from the west coast to about thirty-two degrees east longitude, two-thirds the way across the continent. With the exception of the Desert of Sahara, this territory is about one-third of the inhabited portions of Africa, and larger than the United States, including Alaska. The Congo river is navigable for vessels of five thousand tons to Vivi, one hundred miles from its mouth. Then comes the Livingstone Falls, thirty-two in number, and one hundred and eighty-five miles in length. From the Stanley Pool, at the head of these falls, the Congo is navigable for light

vessels to Stanley Falls, one thousand miles, and
it is estimated, that four thousand miles or more
of navigation is provided by its branches. The
population is forty-nine millions, mostly pagans,
forming a most propitious field for Christianity.
A grammar and dictionary of the Congo language have already been prepared by Mr. H.
Gratton Guinness, of London. Speedily after
the tidings of Stanley's successful journey, Christian hearts in England were stirred. Livingstone
Inland Mission was formed, and the first two
missionaries sailed from Liverpool for the Congo
in January, 1878. Others followed at near
periods. Fifty in all have been engaged in the
work, of whom twenty-six are now in the field.
This mission has recently been transferred to the
American Baptist Missionary Union of our own
country. English Baptists will continue their
work. There are already two mission steamers
on the upper Congo, and one on the lower.
With the contemplated railroad, intercourse and
travel will be comparatively easy.

The International Association, at whose head
is the Catholic King of Belgium, has already
accomplished much, with promise of larger co-
operation. The truly noble Leopold has ex-
pended a million of dollars from his own private
means. In the loss of his only son he adopted
Africa as the child of his heart, and to it he
gives his life's highest powers "

Some time ago the Royal Geographical Society of Great Britain sent out Mr. Joseph Thompson to examine the equatorial region of Eastern Africa. We learn from *Zion's Herald* the following deeply interesting facts which indicate the finger of God :—

"He entered the country from the island of Zanzibar on the eastern coast, with a caravan of a hundred natives bearing his provisions and presents. His journey extended west to Lake Victoria Nyanza. In his exploration within a few degrees of the equator, north and south, he finds, through the different elevations of the land, every kind of temperature, from scorching heat to freezing cold, and an equal variety of fruits and productions of the earth. From his encampment amid tropical ferns he sees skirting the horizon, majestic, abrupt, conical, volcanic peaks, from fourteen to nineteen thousand feet in height, their tops glittering with perennial snow. He finds a brave, intelligent race of manly height, well-formed, with few of the pure negro characteristics. They are savage and ready to fight, but they are equally ready to trade. The country is full of game of all kinds and of the most majestic beasts—the lion, elephant, rhinoceros, zebra, buffalo, etc.—and large portions of the soil very fertile. Traders in ivory, skins and tropical fruits are constantly entering the country in caravans, and government stations are being established at various points. The work of civilization will move slowly because these representatives of it are unfortunate illustrators of a higher form of social and religious life. But these men are opening the way for something better.

Can any Christian doubt the providential intimation of these movements? Is not the finger of God pointing the church towards this long-neglected Continent and its terribly abused peoples? A dispensation of the Gospel has evidently fallen upon all the missionary bodies of Christendom leading them in this direction. They are nearly all now represented in some portion of the land. The American Board, after careful inquiry, and discovering the extensive and invaluable scientific surveys and charts provided by German travelers and scholars, has located a mission in the southern and western portion of the great promontory. The Scotch and the English missions of different denominations are found dotting both coasts and slowly moving into the interior Our own hour has not come too soon. There were many reasons why our very early movement in Liberia seemed to enjoy so feeble a life and so little growth. But a day of larger enterprise is dawning. Who can but pray that the great Head of the Church

will endow the fearless and devoted man — the
Bishop of Africa — who now stands upon its
eastern coast turning his eyes inland, with wisdom in laying the broader foundations of evangelizing instrumentalities among the new tribes
whose lands have already been entered by commercial travelers, and whose intellectual and
religious enlightenment is evidently in the mind
of God as the great outcome of all these more
selfish enterprises!   Men and women will die
and be buried under tropical suns, yet so do men
of the world; but civilization progresses, and
the Kingdom of Christ must certainly come upon
all the earth."

So numerous have been the discoveries
that Africa is almost a new world to us.
We shall need to study its geography over
again, for, in former days,

> " Geographers, in Afric maps
> With savage pictures filled their gaps,
> And o'er unhabitable downs
> Placed elephants for want of towns."

As Bishop Taylor is beginning his missions
in Central Africa, the following will be interesting :—

"Central Africa is high, like an inverted saucer, extending from the Atlantic to the Indian Oceans, with a territory as large as our whole land east of the Rocky Mountains, and with a population of eighty millions. Here are the great lakes, here rise the great rivers of Africa, (Nile, Congo and Zambeze), and here are its highest mountains always covered with snow.

Here is the great kingdom of Uganda, ruled by the suspicious and capricious M'tesa. In 1875 the world was startled and delighted with the message that he wanted his people Christianized, and soon $100,000 were given to the missionary societies of England for this purpose; but the king soon became tired of his new religion."

Since then this king has shown great favor to the missionaries. Sixty-eight persons have been baptized including a number of the royal family. A young chief has accepted Christianity, and sent away all his wives but one. The following is a translation of one verse of "Safe in the Arms of Jesus:"—

"Mu mikono gya ISA:
Emirembe bulijo,
Tetulina entisa:
Tulina esanyu nyo.

KIBUGA, OR RESIDENCE OF THE KING OF UGANDA.

Muwulira edobozi
  Mu Gulu, liyogera,
ISA Ye Mulokozi :
  Ye alina empera.
    Mu mikono gya ISA
      Emirembe bulijo ;
      Tetulina entisa ;
      Tulina esanyu nyo."

I have just learned that King Mtesa is dead. One of his sons has been elected in his stead without the usual bloodshed, owing to the influence of the missionaries. The princess who acts as "king sister" or queen, has embraced Christianity.

I am happy to learn that in Africa the Bible has been translated into eight languages, and parts of the Bible are now published in twenty-six other languages. Twenty-three societies have nearly six hundred missionaries at work in Africa; there are two hundred and fifty thousand Church members, and hundreds of schools have been opened. Still, there is only one missionary to every three hundred and fifty thousand people, and one church member to every eight hundred persons.

One of the wonderful signs of the times is that "the statesmen who composed the African International Conference at Berlin saw the importance of the missionary to the new State and to the whole Congo Basin. They provided in the compact which they entered into not only for the freedom of trade and the development of the resources of the country, but for the 'especial protection' of the religious teacher. The paragraph is worth reproducing :"—

"All the Powers exercising sovereign rights or influence in the aforesaid territories bind themselves to watch over the preservation of the native tribes, and to care for the improvement of the condition of their moral and material wellbeing, and to help in suppressing slavery, and especially the slave trade. They shall, without distinction or creed or nation, protect and favor all religious, scientific, or charitable institutions and undertakings created and organized for the above ends, or which aim at instructing the natives and bringing home to them the blessings of civilization. Christian missionaries, scientists, and explorers, with their followers, property, and collections, shall likewise be the objects of especial protection. Freedom of conscience and religious toleration are expressly guaranteed to the natives, no less than to the subjects (of the sovereign states) and to all foreigners. The free and public exercise of all forms of divine worship, and the right to build churches, temples, and chapels, and to organize religious missions belonging to all creeds, shall not be limited or fettered in any way whatsoever."

Africa has made fearful havoc with its missionaries. In twenty years the English Church Missionary Society sent out eighty-five missionaries to Sierra Leone, two thirds of them died, and fourteen returned home wrecked. In the same time the Wesleyan Missionary Society sent out eighty-six missionaries, half of them died and most of the rest went home half dead.

But remember Christ laid down his precious life for those teeming millions, who are so superstitious that they worship rivers, lakes and mountains, thinking that the gods dwell there, and also snakes, crocodiles and monkeys, thinking that the spirits of their fathers dwell in them. Hundreds of people are killed at the burial of a chief, and sometimes living women are buried in his grave.

The following speech was made before the Missionary Committee in New York, and speaks for itself:—

Bishop Taylor then addressed the committee. He said the subject was a great one. We must fully understand ourselves. Africa was considerable of a place. It covered Liberia, and therefore it was his prerogative to preside in that Conference without being a member thereof; the General Superintendents divide their work among themselves, and after that division each has a certain right within the territory designated which none of the rest would invade. In Africa he would be a Bishop, and need join no Conference. He certainly could not administer the office out of Africa, and no other Bishop could administer in Africa without his consent. As to the right to found missions in Africa, the continent is open to this Society, and it has a right to divide it up into mission fields.

Bishop Taylor then proceeded to set forth his well known views concerning the support of missions. He said he believed in God and man and Methodism, and in all the doctrines and methods of Methodism. There are many millions of Asiatics among whom mission work must be supported by the home Churches. But this need not be the method everywhere. Any man who has a head on him and a heart in him and a pair of legs to carry him around, can be an indigenous, self-supporting agency. He felt that while it was the privilege of this Missionary Committee to found missions wherever they like, he also had the right to use the other method whenever it can be done. He explained that by "self-supporting" missions he meant such as support their ministers from indigenous resources, leaving the contributions of others as a fund for transit and building purposes. Such a plan is nothing new, but precisely what we do at home. Now, this committee has a right to found missions where they like. Such as are founded by them in Africa he purposed to administer as wisely as he could and with the deepest in their success — but for the missions which God enabled him to plant in Africa. He did not want one penny of appropriation — it would only do them harm. He must lay the Gospel granite of these foundations down upon the bed-rock of solid human character. By evident freedom from motives of self-interest he must prove the reality and perfect sincerity of his love for men, and touch in them the principles of hospitality and sympathy. Christ came to our level. He sought to get his leverage in on the bottom level. They went as "lambs among wolves" and it seemed as though the only good prospect was for the wolves. But the disciples came back so exultant with success that they forgot to say anything about the question of support until the Master asked them long after, "lacked ye any thing?" and they replied, "nothing."

When the Missionary Committee were discussing whether they should make an appropriation of money for Africa :—

Bishop Foss suggested that Bishop Taylor might consent if it was explicitly understood that nothing should be applied to salaries.

Bishop Taylor said that those who were going with him were volunteers. None had been asked to go. So many had offered themselves that he had been puzzled how many to take. With much emphasis he said, he was not going as an experiment. They meant to burn the bridges behind them; they meant to make a conquest. "Though I die on the way the thing will be done," was his earnest declaration. As for the appropriation, he did not want it; it would only hamper him.

Bishop Foss said that there seemed to be a little decay among us of true missionary heroism. In many places there is too much anxious questioning about the matter of the precise amount of salary in a given field. It may be that the great God has raised up Bishop Taylor to arouse the heroism of the Church. If it was worth while for Livingstone and Barth and Stanley to make trails of light across the Dark Continent, why not for Bishop Taylor? He wished that just what the Bishop desired should be done.

A VILLAGE IN CENTRAL AFRICA.

There should be no hinderance to his steps. He hoped, however, that Bishop Taylor could consent to the original motion, so as to provide for sudden emergencies. But if Bishop Taylor should object he would object.

According to the wish of Bishop Taylor the appropriation was not made.

The carefulness of the preparation will be seen in the following found in the *Christian Advocate*, N. Y. :—

WILLIAM TAYLOR'S EXPEDITION TO CENTRAL AFRICA.

By the will of God forty or more missionary men and women are preparing for an early departure from their American homes to go to the Yushalange country, five degrees south of the equator. They go to labor among nations unknown to history till reported last January by Lieutenant Wismann, of the German African Geographical Society. When these missionaries shall have settled down in their new fields of labor they will depend entirely on African resources for subsistance, without drawing any salary from home.

Their friends cheerfully send to our Transit Fund the money required for their outfit and passage. The expenses of their African inland traveling have to be paid in cotton cloth and other useful things that the natives can appreciate.

So I propose to give the friends of African evangelization an opportunity to send us the things needful for outfit and inland traveling expenses. I do this because, first, there may be many persons who can send us goods who cannot so readily give us money to buy them; and, second, we do not really know what we shall require for such a journey, and, hence, by this method the Lord can prompt his people to send us the varieties and quantities that he knows we shall need. Leaving, therefore, a margin for the judgment and choice of the donors, I will simply indicate such things as I think we shall need, namely, in the way of dry goods; Middlesex or Washington Mills indigo blue flannel, waterproof cloth for ladies, gossamer underwear, cheap unbleached cotton cloth in large quantities, Turkey red, blue cotton drill, cotton hose, hammocks, handkerchiefs, etc. Sundries: Pins, needles, thread, buttons, buckles, etc. Note-paper, envelopes, slates, five by seven inches, in large quantity; lead and slate pencils; matches in tin boxes; pocket-knives, hoes, spades, shovels, etc.; washing and toilet soap; small, cheap musical instruments and mirrors, etc. A hand printing press, suitable for octavo sheets, with paper to suit.

Groceries: Liebig's extract of meat, corned

beef in cans, and a variety of preserved meats, fruits, vegetables, milk, etc.

Any of these things may be sent by the donors in large or small quantities marked as follows: "For William Taylor's African Expedition," care of Messrs. Baker, Pratt & Co., 17 Bond Street, New York. For further information address me or Richard Grant, 181 Hudson Street, New York.

We have contracted for good waterproof tents to cost $20 each. Any person wishing to contribute a tent, and have his name written on it, may send us that amount and indicate that it is to pay for a tent, and it will be attended to till the tents are all taken, and the excess will go for passage of missionaries. Our big tent for worship will cost $52. Who will be the donor of that?

Humbly submitted in the name of the Lord, by his servant, WILLIAM TAYLOR.

New York, Nov. 18, 1884.

The widow of the late Bishop Simpson paid for the big tent for worship, in the behalf of her lamented husband; to be called "The Bishop Simpson Tent."

At this time Bishop Taylor was busy accepting his missionaries and getting ready his supplies. Meanwhile many rumors were

abroad about this great movement; some for
and some against it.   One man wrote as follows: "We shall see what we shall see.
We confess we don't take much stock in the
eccentric Taylor's plans.   He has a heart for
his work but needs a head to control his
heart.   To throw himself against the collec-
tive wisdom and the traditions of the Church,
and thus to undertake the evangelization of
Africa, as the independent fighter of a western regiment once said, on his own hook,
seems to be wonderfully like the fool-hardi-
ness of a crank."

Zion's Herald took a calm, candid view
and said, "He is a man of God, of an
heroic mold, and full of resources as well as
faith.   There is no occasion for any of his
many friends to fear that he will lack abun-
dant pecuniary aid as it may be required.
Already he has supplies for a year, and an
open and direct line of sympathy with thousands of appreciative supporters."

Bishop Taylor, having finished his prepa-
rations, as far as he could, bade adieu to this
country December 13, 1884, and sailed to
Liverpool, where he is well known.   He
found many friends in England who were

very liberal with their offerings and very much pleased with his great *missionary movement*. On his way to Liverpool he sent a letter to the Book Committee of the Church that sent him out, as follows :—

To the Book Committee of the Methodist Episcopal Church:—

Dear Brethren,—I wish respectfully to call your thoughtful attention to the status, relationship and rights of our Missionary Episcopacy. The points of difference between a Missionary Bishop and any one of our regular Board of Bishops pertain not to the status and functions of the episcopal office, but simply to minor conditions pertaining to their respective fields of episcopal jurisdiction. By the action of the Board of Bishops, under the Discipline, the field of each bishop for one year is defined and limited and officially announced in the plan of Episcopal Visitation. By the action of the General Conference a foreign continent is assigned to their Missionary Bishop, without time limitations or any authoritative interferences whatever, during good behavior, except that of subsequent action by a General Conference. Their Missionary Bishop is invested with the same episcopal functions in Africa as those of the regular College of Bishops in their fields of episcopal jurisdiction :

and as none of them have the right to go into the
field of another to exercise episcopal functions
without the consent of the incumbent, so no one
of them has a right to exercise episcopal functions in Africa without the consent of its bishop.
As we have two methods financially of founding
churches in America — first, the primary self-
supporting method as exemplified in about nine-
tenths of our home Churches and the Churches of
the South India Conference, and second, the
more modern method of founding Churches by
the appointment of men and the appropriation
of money for their support, under the auspices
of our Missionary Society — so under the late
amendments of the Discipline the first as well as
the second of these methods has become legitimate in foreign countries under the law of the
Church.

As the episcopal supervision of our regular
Board of Bishops applies alike to both these
methods and to the Church founded under
them, so the episcopal supervision of the Missionary Bishop applies in Africa alike to both
these methods and to the Churches founded under
them. As the home Bishops are not the em-
ployees of the Missionary Society, nor hence dependent on said Society for their support, so the
Missionary Bishop is not an employee of the Missionary Society, nor hence dependent on that
Society for his support. The regular Bishops

and the Missionary Bishops are alike the episcopal servants of the Church, under the authority
of the General Conference; hence, both are alike
entitled to a support directly from the Church
through " the Episcopal Fund."   " The laborer
is worthy of his hire," to be paid by the party
employing him.   When the Missionary Society
employ a missionary they pay him " his hire."
When a self-supporting Church, at home or
abroad, accepts the appointment of a minister,
they thereby assume the responsibility of his
support.

But when a Missionary Bishop, or founder of
Churches in foreign countries, goes forth on his
own account he must make tents, or otherwise
provide for his own support, or, if sent forth
under competent authority, should be supported
by the body under whose authority he is sent.
These facts are so simple and self-evident as not
to require argument to support them.

Now, my dear brethren, I write thus, not so
much for my own sake, as for the sake of the
office of a Missionary Episcopacy. God is leading
our Church in this direction to increase her efficiency for conquering the continents of heathenism in foreign lands; hence the propriety of in-
troducing this subject now.   The Missionary
Committee, at its recent session, tacitly conceded
the facts I have stated, hence did not, by appropriations nor otherwise, establish a claim to juris-

diction over me, nor over any portion of Africa beyond, nor over the self-supporting Churches that God may enable me to establish in Africa. They made simply their usual appropriations to Liberia yet have, of course, the undisputed right to found in Africa, by their own favorite method, as many missions as they may elect to found and to exercise jurisdiction over all such, but not over any self-supporting Churches. My term of official service for the Church may date from the day of my departure for Africa — December 13th inst. The amount of compensation I leave to your own godly judgment of the sacrifice and service to be rendered.

The traveling expenses of our Bishops in foreign countries are paid from the missionary treasury. As in the past, so in the future, the Lord willing, I will pay my own traveling expenses in all my foreign work, and draw nothing from the missionary treasury, yet attend to their branch of my work with no less fidelity on that account.

Please give me an official report of your decision, and inform me when, and on whom, and for what amount I may draw.

Address me by mail at St. Paul de Loanda, West Coast of Africa. I remain, dear brothers,

Your humble servant,

(Signed), WILLIAM TAYLOR.

S. S. City of Berlin, Dec. 20, 1884.

It is just to say that this Committee had an honest difference of opinion on this subject and sent back a candid reply, that, in their judgment his support would legitimately come from the Missionary Committee. I suppose the matter will remain unsettled till the next General Conference. And I beg the true friends of Bishop Taylor not to stir up strife, nor manifest any unkind feelings toward any parties. Bishop Taylor is amply provided for in the affections and liberal offerings of the people, and it will take no special pleading to furnish him all the money that he needs, either from England or America, or from Australia either. The wealth of three continents is under contribution to support him when it is necessary.

Since writing this I have learned that the friends of Bishop Taylor, in Sidney, New South Wales, Australia, have sent about $485 to Richard Grant, for the evangelization of Africa. So the ends of the earth have their eyes open to this great work to supply all its needs.

At the same time there are so many calls for missionaries, and so many have been sent out, and so many are getting ready to go, and so much money is needed, not only to pay their passage, but also to buy land on which to build schools, colleges or chapels, both in India, South America and Africa, and with the treasury already overdrawn four hundred and fifty dollars, I say there is now a loud call *for a million dollars for each of these Continents.* As many of God's stewards are looking round to find some safe way of investing God's money in their possession, where it will pay dividends from the Bank of Faith through all eternity, they will do well to turn their attention in this direction. For their special benefit I put in the following :—

FORM OF BEQUEST.

I give and bequeath unto "The Transit and Building Fund Society of Bishop William Taylor's Self-Supporting Missions," a corporation duly organized under the laws of the State of New York at the City of New York, in said State, the sum of Dollars to be applied to the uses of said Society.

To what better use can we put our money than to pay the passage of those missionaries who are willing to live and labor among the heathen for whom Christ died? Can you tell? The Transit and Building Fund is to pay the passage of missionaries and to give them an outfit. The Loan Fund is to buy land and help to erect buildings thereon, as the case may be, and this money is to be paid back to the corporation as soon as convenient, and loaned to other parties.

For instance, when Mr. Grant's daughter was going out to Concepcion, South America, it was decided that land must be bought and buildings erected, that would cost, at least, five thousand, five hundred dollars. This suggested the need of a Loan Fund, and Brother Grant started that fund by giving that five thousand, five hundred dollars out of his own pocket. The next time the corporation met they were so pleased with the matter that they subscribed enough to make it up to twelve thousand dollars.

Since then they have loaned two thousand dollars to Rev. J. P. Gilliland, to help to buy land and erect a school building at Iquique. And so they propose to go on until they have a FREEHOLD FOOTING all over their mission fields.

i

Who will make the first investment of
$100,000? Reader, what does the Master
say to you in this case? What will he say
to you at the great day of final account?
Act so that he will say, "Well done, good
and faithful servant, thou hast been faithful
over a few things, I will make thee ruler over
many things, enter thou into the joy of thy
Lord."

The *Congregationalist* of Boston is inclined
to wonder why the apostle of self-support,
who is leading out so many missionaries to
live among heathens, and to live upon them,
too, should ask for support, and wonders why
he should not do as his fellow-workers are to
do.

I would rather Bishop Taylor should speak
for himself. But we may observe that, as
the Church has taken him away from his
chosen work, and from the sale of his books,
and chosen his work for him, and sent him
into the hardest missionary field of the
world, that, therefore, he had a right to expect that that same church, and not the Missionary Society, should give him a support.
But we may differ in our judgment till the
next General Conference, when the combined

wisdom of the Church will set this matter right.

Many were disposed to find fault with William Taylor and his African movement, but then the sober common sense of the church will come to the rescue. I hope the special friends of Bishop Taylor will keep cool, and not hinder the cause by unkind or unjust remarks. I am much pleased with the following.

Rev. Frederick Merrick writes as follows :—

"There is something unseemly in the discussion which is going on in reference to the movement of Bishop Taylor. Better all betake ourselves to prayer. Let prayer be made without ceasing that God would have the Bishop and his devoted band under His special care, and that He would open to them great doors and effectual for the preaching of His Word. Let all pray that no strange fire be found to mingle in the warmth of the controversy, and that no unjust prejudices be formed that shall in any way tend to hinder the work of God. Let prayer be made that the church may not abuse this unusual movement by finding in it an excuse for its parsimonious giving; but that, instead, its heart may be stirred to far greater liberality. And let not this band be forgotten in the distribution to the saints.

God manifestly has some great and gracious purpose toward Africa. How wonderful the discoveries in that continent within the last few decades! The discovery of America was hardly more wonderful. The movement of Bishop Taylor seems, in its moral grandeur, wondrously in harmony with the general movement. Who doubts there was a Divine guidance in the movements of Livingstone, Stanley and others in opening the continent to the Christian world? And why should it be thought a thing incredible that God should have had a hand in the strange selection of this somewhat anomalous agency for occupying a portion, and a very important portion, of the territory for Christ? Certainly it can hardly be said to have been of man's devising. It seems to have taken some by surprise who might have been expected to have been the chief agents in directing the movement. What if such find some difficulty in adjusting themselves to so unsuspected an order of things? It is hardly safe to discard, as some seem inclined to do, the idea of Divine interposition from an apparent lack of wisdom in the movement. God sometimes finds it necessary to teach His people how insufficient they are of themselves to carry forward his work. They are prone to forget that it is not by might, nor by power, but by His spirit the work of saving souls is accomplished. He must choose His own instruments and methods. 'The foolishness of God is wiser than men.' 'So then neither is he that planteth anything, nor he that watereth, but God that giveth the increase.' It may be well for all to act cautiously, lest, peradventure some, unwittingly, be found fighting against God. 'Lord, increase our faith!'

Let those opposed to self-supporting missions redouble their donations to the regular mission work, for there is great need of it, and most, undoubtedly, might and *ought* to do it; and let those who are disposed to commend this African mission for its trust to providential support, inquire prayerfully if they have not providentially been given the means needed to meet the exigencies of this work, and so made, in a measure responsible for its success. True faith works—works by love. With a burning zeal for the glory of God and the redemption of the greatly-abused continent, with the utmost sincerity and earnestness, let each inquire, 'Lord, what wilt Thou have me to do?' Holy Father, richly baptize Thy people with the spirit of the wisdom and power of a divine love! Theirs shall be the benefit, Thine the glory. Amen!'"

Rev. J. O. Knowles, D. D., writes some kind and timely things. It is just like his kind and generous heart to express himself as follows:—

"What is the cause of this latest sensation?
Simply this: Bishop Taylor has found a company
of royal men and women, who, with himself,
propose to plant the Gospel in the heart of the
· Dark Continent,' and have settled in their
minds that they will not ask the over-burdened
missionary treasury for a penny; whereupon, the
cowardice latent in human nature wakes up a
little and paradoxically whispers, 'This whole
business will dampen missionary zeal and dry up
missionary contributions!' Cowardice is generally silly and puts on its tallest 'fool's cap'
when it hints such an absurdity. As though
the great Church of Christ is shut up to but one
method! Or, if two could be found, they must
be self-destructive! Ought the Mission Board
to refuse a check for $100,000 because it does
not come in the regular collections? Or, if a
trader on the coast of Guinea should go to
preaching the Gospel without asking them for
salary or authority, ought they by telegraph and
messengers to notify him to stop, lest missionary
collections should 'dry up.'

The 'Pauline method' concerning which some
are displaying a little innocent but unnecessary
ignorance, was simply 'by all means to save
some.' Paul, to do a part of his work, earned
his own bread and asked no authority from the
church; but did he tumble down the church by
so doing? He 'took letters' when he needed

them, and pay too, — at times; and raised missionary money until he could honestly boast of it. He is the author of the system of "weekly offerings" in the churches. Bishop Taylor does not assail the Missionary Society; he simply sets himself to try *one* of Paul's methods. If he succeeds — as God grant he may!—will it undo the work of the last fifty years? Does civilization stand still and, rot when the pioneer, with salt pork and hard-tack in his knapsack, goes into the wilderness? Surely the independent explorer prevents the rot of civilization and sets all its tides to pulsing along the trails he blazes. Let Bishop Taylor and his brave company succeed, and it will stimulate the flow of missionary contributions as all the 'appeals' of the last twenty years have not been able to do. May not the inspiration of this dash, self-sacrifice and faith quicken the stinted flow we have spent so much time and shed so much ink in deploring? This new movement on Africa will not hinder our general missionary work; but this controversy springing up will do so, and the shallowest practical wisdom can see it.

'Observer,' who, in his New York letter printed in the *Herald* of March 4, hints that Africa may prove 'our Soudan,' must remember that the fault in Egypt was not in the 'Pauline method' of Gen. Gordon, but in the stupidity, fussiness and incapacity of the regulars. He seems to be mildly 'going for' Bishop Taylor; but his illustration logically reflected upon the Missionary Board.   Let the whole church pray for Bishop Taylor and the heroes who attend him in this truly Christian missionary enterprise, and let this praying help the whole church to wake up to the duty offering, and fill the missionary treasury that we may push our organized work along the track of personal devotion ! "

The latest news from South America is that the government of Chili has thrown off the incubus of Catholicism by disestablishing it as a State Church.   So that Mr. Taylor's Misssions and Christian schools will help to save this people from infidelity.

I learn, also, that such is the prosperity of our College at Santiago that the income from tuition and board, last year, was $25,000. So that this institution is well prepared to support itself.   Many leading families in that region utterly refuse to have their children taught in the Catholic church.

Rev. J. W. Hamilton, who was a member of the last General Conference, writes as follows to the *Northern Christian Advocate:*—

"The letter of William Taylor to the Book Committee, will open the eyes of the Church more and more as the students of the Discipline and the General Conference journals come to take the time which the African Bishop found on the high seas, to look into this subject. There is but a single provision in the law of the Church now existing that can be made to apply to this case of William Taylor, and that is to be found in the changes of the restrictive rule begun in the General Conference of 1856, and consummated by the action of the annual conferences held afterwards and voting in favor of the change. All legislation relating to Bishop Burns or Bishop Roberts was special and could not apply to any other Bishop, or Bishops without being revised by another special enactment.

The status of an African Bishop, as determined by Dr. Buckley, editor of the *New York Christian Advocate*, who has a special acuteness for jurisprudence, which is usually interested in bringing matters to a more reliable issue, is therefore purely gratuitous and not statutory. The precedent which he would apply to Bishop Taylor, will no more rightfully apply to him than the law enacted at the same time for the Liberia Conference, will now apply to that body. It was resolved that "The Liberia Conference shall be under the general supervision of the Methodist Episcopal Church, as our foreign missions now are." But the General Conference of 1868 made the Liberia Conference in point of legal privilege as the New York East. Since the African Bishop is no longer " off color," why should he then be off grade? The Conference in Liberia is entitled to as big a Bishop as the Conference in New York. This was not wholly unknown or out of mind at the General Conference in Philadelphia last May, as may appear when the latest developments make known all that was said " behind the scenes."

The bishopric, whether in America or in Africa, is both an *office* and an *order*. As an office it is jurisdictional; as an order it possesses the unquestioned and unlimited right within the law to confer orders. In Africa we limit the office to Africa, but the order is neither limited nor restrained, it may run out into the whole world.

> ' The currents sweep the Old World,
>   The currents sweep the New.
> The wind will blow, the dawn will glow
>   Ere thou hast sailed them through.'

William Taylor is as much a Bishop, in the nature and grade of his order, as the Bishop of London. All he needs to widen his jurisdiction is a vote of the General Conference; no one would certainly claim that he must receive new prerogatives, by being a second time ordained. His is simply a diocean episcopacy."

He then compares this case of William Taylor with that of Bishop Coke, and closes by saying :—

" The circumstances of the restrictions differ of course in the case of Thomas Coke from those in the case of William Taylor, but the powers remaining under the restrictions differ in no particular. Thomas Coke came down from the General Superintendency to a diocean episcopacy, as William Taylor may some day go up from the diocean superintendency to the general episcopacy."

In writing the life of this wonderful man of God it has been suggested to me that William Taylor was, to all intents and purposes, an Apostle, sent by God to open and establish missions in all the earth, before he was elected a Bishop; and inasmuch as we all know that an apostleship is higher than a bishopric, then in this sense, it was a condecension on his part to accept this office of a Bishop. But as he did not give up the apostleship to become a Bishop, therefore, he is now, in the providence of God, both an Apostle and a Bishop.

And thus he is honored by earth and

heaven; for while man made him a Bishop, God made him an Apostle.

And as God has some special favors to bestow upon the sons of Ham, on the continent of Africa, he has raised up this apostolic man and given him full authority from earth and heaven to go forth to scatter heavenly light amid the hellish darkness that has so long pervaded that sin-cursed land. And having prepared and sent forth this special minister for this special purpose he will especially sustain and prosper both him and his colaborers in this heaven-born enterprise. So let all doubts be forever banished from all minds, God is in the field, leading on his militant hosts to certain victories, till "all the ends of the earth shall see the salvation of God."

Let us pray for this and labor for it, and give of our money, and thus help on the conquest of the world. I am glad to find that reinforcements are forthcoming already. Ministers are feeling that they must go to Africa, and money is being raised to send them out.

CHAPTER VII.

BISHOP TAYLOR IN AFRICA AND HIS COMPANY FOLLOWING ON.

The following letter from *The Christian Standard* speaks for itself, from Bishop Taylor :—

MONROVIA, Liberia, Feb. 5, 1885.

REV. E. I. D. PEPPER :—

Dear Bro, —I arrived here by the steamship Gaboon, on Thursday, 7.30 P. M., the 22nd Jan. (ult.) I preached in our Church here the same night to a small congregation. On Friday at 4 P. M. I preached in Krootown, in Miss Mary Sharp's school house. Except Saturdays I have held two special services daily ever since that at Krootown, at 4.30 P. M., and to crowds in our Church at Monrovia at 7.30 P. M., and meantime have held the Conference of six days, including Sabbath. We have had, and are having a precious work of salvation in the Entire Sanctification of believers; and the conversion of many sinners, I don't know how many. We have from twenty to thirty seekers forward each night, for ten days past and a few of them saved at each meeting. Some of them shout all over the house, and some from house to house nearly all over the town. Sister Amanda Smith is here at the front and as usual doing grand service. Monrovia is built on a peninsula about two miles long and a mile wide, a high uneven hill, iron stone gravel, and huge boulders, basaltic, with seven or eight per cent. of iron.

The water from wells is good, the climate salubrious and equable. It seems to be a healthy place. The people seem to be in good health, but few of them ill, most of them in very moderate circumstances financially, but in the main they dress well, and present a good appearance. I enjoy this climate, eat well, sleep well, work hard, and keep close to Jesus. I have great cause of gratitude to God, and nothing to complain about, and no disposition to be dissatisfied with God or man. God's ways are in accord with His infinite wisdom, righteousness, and love. Man's ways accord with the various standards of their education, the perversities of their nature, and with the transformations of grace in those who are saved, but, so far as they touch me personally, I have no complaint to lay against any, but am a debtor alike to civilized and savage people for per-

sonal kindness according to their opportunity.
Next to my supreme love to God, I love mankind, and live to honor God and do good to
man. I will (D. V.) spend next Sabbath at
Virginia, up the St. Paul's river, preaching there
through the Sabbath, and on Monday and Tuesday visit a few other stations on that river. On
Wednesday we expect our English steamer
going south, by which I hope to get a passage
to Great Bassa about eighty miles south. I will
have spent a month in Liberia, if I get passage
by the S. S. Nubia, on the 22nd inst., on which
I hope to join my band of heroic men, women,
and children who were to sail from New York
on the 22nd of January, the day of my arrival
here. Glory to God. Your Brother,

WM. TAYLOR.

I find still another letter from the same :—

MONROVIA, Liberia, Feb. 6.

My Dear Brethren,—I report progress by saying that I arrived here at 7.30 P M., on Thursday, 22d ult., the day my people were to sail
from New York. I preached that night in our
church here. I had written our people in this
place that I wanted to preach in Monrovia a
week before Conference. By the special Providence of God, I arrived just one week before

Conference, and found the people assembled and waiting for me. Although the steamer to stop here did not arrive for nearly a week late, I arrived on time exactly by a steamer that was not to stop here, but did stop solely for my accommodation. So I stepped in on time, as usual.

I have a delightful home with President Henry Cooper and his family, from Virginia, but many years resident here. I have the best of accommodations every way, and not more than one or two mosquitoes a week. No fleas, no gnats, no bedbugs, nor big-bugs, nor humbugs, that I wot of. The climate is delightful.

I have been holding from two to three services daily for over two weeks that I have been here, besides holding the Liberia Conference. We have had a pleasant session of the Conference,—a number of Christians sanctified wholly, and for the last ten days we have daily from fifteen to thirty seekers of pardon at the front, and many have professed conversion to God. At almost any hour, day or night, we hear in the homes of the people, in all parts of the town, the triumphant shouts of new-born souls.

Sister Amanda Smith is with us, in the power and demonstration of the Spirit, as usual. God has yet much work for her to do in this land, and she will follow His orders.

I will (D. V.) work a few days at different stations up the St. Paul's River, and a few days in the Grand Bassa country, about eighty miles south of this point; then join the steamship *Nubia*, on which I hope to meet my heroic men, women, and children, from New York.

Glory to God for what He has done for us, and for what He is going to do here and in South Central Africa!

Sister Mary Sharp is doing a good work here in the Kroo tribe of natives. I have been preaching daily to them. Your brother,

WILLIAM TAYLOR.

Miss Mary A. Sharp sends the following account :—

She says: "Bishop Taylor arrived on January 22nd after dark. He has preached twice a day every week day, every afternoon at Krootown to a native audience. We are having a wonderful work of grace there. Yesterday a powerfully built man said: 'Last night I began to pray,—Me say Lord Jesus, me don't know you. I have stood about you and I come to you. Now me beg you to save me.' In the church at Monrovia the altar is crowded with seekers for pardon and seekers for holy hearts.—Yesterday, the 29th, Conference convened. All the members were present but two.

The Bishop presided. After the session he
dined hurriedly, and then went down to Krootown to my bamboo church. On the way back
he met some one pressing him to go and help
another into the light. Then he preached again
until 10 o'clock at the church in Monrovia.
The fever will have no chance at him with such
prodigious work. God is with us. Glory to
His name !"—*Northern Advocate.*

While Bishop Taylor was sailing from
Liverpool to Liberia his missionary band
were directing their steps toward the city of
New York. Brother Withey had been
there some time, assisting Brother Grant in
getting ready the many needed supplies.

Special meetings, for a Pentecostal baptism, were appointed in the Carrol Park
Methodist Church, Brooklyn, whose pastor,
Rev. Mr. McBride and people very kindly
furnished homes for these pilgrims. Rev.
J. D. Griffin presided. The ever blessed
Holy Ghost rested upon the people from
time to time. God manifested himself in
great power in these meetings, many were
sanctified and some were converted.
Heaven's glory filled the place.

Here was Rev. Ross Taylor the Bishop's

son, and his family, who had just arrived
from California, where he had just been ordained. The youngest missionary in this
group was only six weeks old. Here was
Brother Withey and wife and four children,
also Dr. Levi Johnson and Delia Reese, of
the Society of Friends. Here was Miss Dr.
Myers, of the Boston University, who was
willing, with the rest, to tramp a thousand
miles into the wilds of Africa. Indeed the
spirit of martyrdom possessed this whole
company; they were all willing to lay down
their lives for Christ. Indeed they were in-
spired of the Holy Ghost to make this sacrifice, and of course God blessed the offering
and sent down upon them the baptismal fire.
Especially on the last night of the meeting
the church was crowded and the meeting
continued till near the midnight hour. Hundreds were thrilled in hearing the testimonies
of this heroic company. After a few hours'
rest they met the next morning upon the
wharf. It was the bitter cold morning of the
twenty-second of January, 1885, but their
hearts were all aglow with heavenly love.

The following letter is so complete and
comprehensive that I make room for it, as it

is the testimony of an eye witness who is a noted minister of the Methodist Episcopal Church :—

·'At 9 o'clock upon a cold winter morning twenty-nine men and women, with sixteen children, embarked upon the *City of Montreal* with their glad faces set toward Congo-land. It was the largest company of new missionaries that ever sailed at any one time from American or English shores within the knowledge of the writer. It should form an epoch in the history of missions. They represented many different States and diverse callings. Preachers, evangelists, teachers, physicians, printers, farmers, carpenters, stenographers, were of the number. They go out under the leadership of Rishop Taylor. After three days in Liverpool they depart for Loando, on the west coast of Africa, where the leaders of the expedition have made preparation for their arrival and for their further journey, which includes one thousand miles on foot. They were a happy, devoted, determined band. It was a precious privilege to take them by the hand, look into their noble faces, and to hear their cheering words. Their weapons were both carnal and spiritual. But the rifles and shot-guns were for game in their self-support, and the five thousand Bibles to m⌐ke captive the hearts of men for the

Lord Jesus. Cloth and various other articles for traffic, a printing-press, blankets, etc., constituted their baggage. The youngest outgoing missionary the writer ever beheld was the six-weeks old baby.

It was one of six, all under fourteen years of age. Mr. Taylor, son of the Bishop, was accompanied by Mrs. Taylor and four children. They desire to show to the natives of interior Africa a Christian household. God grant they may arrive at their destination in unbroken numbers. The entire company was photographed on deck. Many friends came to bid them God-speed. There were the usual tender farewells and tears — the sorrow seeming to belong to those who were left behind, the joy to those who departed. The final separation came. As the bitter north wind blew, and the steamer crushed through the ice, the parted company, on shore and on vessel, united in singing the " Sweet Bye and Bye," and " Praise God, from whom all blessings flow," and amid the waving of handkerchiefs and the shouts of adieus the dear ones were lost to view. And the readers of these simple words that are written with wet eyes will lift up a prayer that the good God of heaven will preserve these men and women and their little ones on the stormy deck, on the long march, and in their future home in Congo-land.

Among the names are those of the Rev. C. L.

Davenport, Mr. and Mrs. Withey, H. C. M'Kinley, Louis Johnson, Charles M. M'Lean, Charles W. Gordon, Miss Delia Reese, Charles L. Miller, C. A. Ratcliff, H. M. Willis, Charles G. Rudolph, W. H. Meade and wife, S. O. Meade and wife, F. B. Northam, Dr. Mary R. Meyers, L. D. Johnson, George B. Mackey, Mr. and Mrs. Taylor.

They go upon the greatest missionary enterprise which the world of to-day presents — grander than any that can come after on the earth's wide surface.

Congo-land is sacred ground. Missionary graves are already there. The sainted James Telford leads the list, one of the countless men prepared for the Master by Mr. Moody. At a farewell meeting in London, Telford exclaimed: "I go gladly on this mission, and shall rejoice if only I may give my body as one of the stones to pave the road into interior Africa, and my blood to cement the stones together, so that others may pass over into Congo-land." Within six months the unconscious prophecy was fulfilled, and the peaceful, joyous, dying words were: "Tell — my — dear — mother — I am — going home."

May the sorrowing souls who have given their dear ones to this far-off land be consoled with the reflection that the all-loving Father and the heaven-home are as near to Congo-land as to London or New York."

GIDEON DRAPER.

For many years I have felt that if the heathen world was ever to be taken for Christ, we must move out among them in Christian colonies, large enough to make an impression upon them; but little thought that I should live to see it. I am glad also that a number of whole families have gone over, so that they can show the heathen how to train their families. These Christian children will be a band of missionaries if they live, and a band of angels if they die. I rejoice that the parents refused to leave them behind. Let them live and die together.

Just before sailing Miss Myers heard of the death of her father, but she would not stay; amid blinding tears she bade adieu to her native home. Indeed, many of them had to tear themselves away from friends that were dear as their lives; but they loved Christ dearer than life. Dr. A. Lowrey gives the following interesting account:—

" The composition of this group of missionaries seemed to us singularly complete and well-proportioned — one or more thoroughly trained financiers, two physicians (one male and one female), two or more experienced school teachers, mechanics, farmers, trained musicians, vocal and instrumental, some highly educated, some not, but all intelligent, some gifted evangelists, some women like Priscilla able to teach Apollos the way of the Lord more perfectly, and others like Lydia adapted to entertain the apostles Two of the company were Friend Quakers — Delia Reese and Levi D. Johnson, M. D. A peculiar interest clustered around these persons, as they were the first-fruits of the modern missionary revival among the Friends. Accordingly, David Updegraff, of Ohio, and Elizabeth Farnum, of Philadelphia, both persons of great prominence among the Friends, were there with beaming faces to see them set sail, and say to them so sweetly, ' Levi, I bid thee farewell; ' and then kissing Delia Reese and saying, ' Delia, I bid thee farewell.'

We were especially interested in Elizabeth Farnum. She has long been a preacher among the Friends, and is now quite advanced in life. The vessel was advertised to leave at nine o'clock. The morning of the twenty-second was intensely cold; but Elizabeth was there — not only on the dock, but on the vessel down in the cabin with a heart as jubilant as a girl of sixteen and a smile sweet as that of an angel. She was the last to leave when the bell rang, and the order was given to go ashore.

The time of parting had now come. It was a supreme moment. They on board and we on shore stood face to face in the severely cold air and strong wind. The missionaries with full hearts began to sing the favorite old hymn,—

' The birds without barn or storehouse are fed,
From them let us learn to trust for our bread;
His saints, what is fitting, shall ne'er be denied,
So long as 'tis written, " The Lord will provide;" ' '

with the stimulating chorus,

' Yes, I will rejoice.'

When the vessel moved, those on board and those on shore with one accord struck up the plaintive strain, ' In the Sweet Bye and Bye,' and then with waving hats and handkerchiefs, in the midst of blinding tears, we bade them, and they bade us a long and loving farewell."

Tens of thousands of Christians remembered them in their prayers, and then Elder Brother Jesus was very near, and the Comforter, the Holy Ghost, filled their souls.

God and the good people of America not only supplied their passage money, but also funds to give them a good outfit. Bishop

Taylor sent word to his treasurer, Richard Grant, that the people of England would make up what was lacking; and England did nobly.

So that this party not only took with them twenty-five knapsacks and as many haver-sacks, and twelve rifles and as many sewing machines, the gift of E. Remington & Sons, but also one hundred pounds of phonetic type, and many other essentials, but they took also provisions, as canned meat and other necessaries to last them one year.

So that it was not so wild and fanatical a project as some seem to suppose. The future will tell. God will make known his good pleasure, and the ends of the earth shall be converted to Christ, and

' His kingdom stretch from shore to shore,
Till moons shall wax and wane no more.'

The following letter will be read with interest and profit :—

STEAMER CITY OF MONTREAL, January 31.

Dear————, ————The blessed Spirit is with us, and has wonderfully sustained and kept us — soul and body. We had a hard storm. This ship has made 108 trips, and the sailors say they

never saw such a storm before. Had not God
stayed the waves, we should all have been
drowned; but He held them in control.

We have had good meetings in the cabin, and
there have been several conversions among the
sailors and steerage passengers. One night, I
think one hundred rose to their feet, signifying
that they wanted to go with us to glory. How
eagerly they listened to the story of Jesus! God
bless and save them! I love their souls.

I find it sweet to trust in Jesus. How glad I
have been that I had the witness in my heart to
my salvation, and that the blood cleansed me
from all sin, and I was ready to meet God. If
we would have peace in our hearts in the time of
trouble, we must secure it when there is calm.
Glory to His name for the precious blood that
has cleansed me from all sin and made one so
vile as I as white as snow. He has taken away
the fear of death, and all worry and fretfulness
and impatience, and given me His sweet Spirit.
He is ever holding this out to a dying world,
and whosoever will, may take the great salvation. We must yield ourselves to Him — body,
soul and spirit,— and then the Holy Ghost re-
veals what the dear Saviour is to us,— a perfect
salvation, a perfect redemption, and perfect freedom from all sin.

Yours in Jesus,

MRS. W. H. MEAD.

S. S. CITY OF MONTREAL, Jan. 30, 1885.

Dear Bro., — Everything has been in our favor thus far. Praise the Lord! We had an accident Wednesday morning, but the Lord sustained us. On account of the heavy gale blowing Tuesday afternoon and night, the engineer slackened his power in the engines, because the wind was carrying us along so nicely; but it was blowing so hard that it sent the surging sea over the stern with such volume and terrific force, that it crushed the panels of the cabin-door, covering the stairway leading to the rooms below. The water entered almost every room, especially Bro. Taylor's. Some one shouted "All hands forward!" I heard the shout and thought the side of the vessel was crushed in. Everyone was cool and deliberate. None of us screamed, nor were any of us frightened. About half a dozen of us set to work dipping the water out of the rooms with pails, tin boxes, etc., while the seamen covered the exposed places with canvas.

The weather was quite warm, and for that reason no one suffered very much on account of the accident. A wave snapped both stanchions (iron, six inches thick), which hold the life-boat; another swept over the deck and washed the boatswain overboard; but while passing over he took hold, and was saved. Two of his ribs were crushed, and he is lying ill; but will recover.

Mrs. Withey has been very sick, and is now

very weak. The whole family have been very sick, but have almost recovered. Bro. Taylor's second youngest child was very sick, but is well now. Bro. McKinley is in the worst condition of all. Mrs. Willis is very feeble. The children suffered least of any from sea-sickness. If anyone says that children are a burden, tell them that the children have been the cause of less trouble than the grown ones. "Suffer little children to come unto Me," saith the Lord.

I have been well, and enjoyed the voyage very much, especially the storm.

Will write more when I reach Loando, if possible. I hope you will remember me in your prayers. I remain,

Your brother in Christ,

C. G. RANDOLPH.

LIVERPOOL, ENG., Feb. 3, 1885.

Dear Bro. Lowrey,— Our voyage on the *City of Montreal* was somewhat an eventful one, and was completed in a little less than eleven days, — leaving New York on Thursday, January 22, at 9 A. M., and reaching Liverpool at three o'clock on Sunday morning, February 1. At the beginning we organized for the voyage, electing Brother A. E. Withey, President, and Dr. Levi Johnson, Secretary. On the first day, before night, many of the party became sea-sick ; others held out well until the second day, when very few appeared at the table. Names of those who appeared at every meal during the voyage, so far as I could see, were Bros. Willis, McLean, Ross Taylor, Dodson and Sister Reese. Others were slightly sick, and stayed away occasionally; but before the end of the trip, most all appeared but Bros. Davenport, Mackey and McKinley, the latter of whom is so disabled by continual prostration that he will have to remain in England for a time.

We apppointed prayer-service and preaching three times daily, preaching at 2.30 P. M., and prayer-service at 6.30 A. M., and 7 o'clock P. M. The prayer-services were kept up constantly, but on account of sickness the afternoon service was not held some days.

On the first Sabbath, Bros. Gordon and Dodson were appointed to call on the captain and ascertain if he intended to hold services on board as was advertised. The captain replied that he had discontinued it, whereupon we asked the privilege of holding services in the saloon and inviting the ship's crew and steerage passengers, which was granted, but he refused to allow us on any condition to go into the steerage apartment and preach, fearing riot, there being many Catholics there. We held our meetings in the saloon as usual, and from that time continued preaching and prayer-service in the evening, at which several were converted, and during their progress one professed santification,—a very fine young Irishman from Dublin, with whom our party were very much impressed. He seemed a young man of great promise, his appearance and bearing being very attractive.

A very interesting occurrence during the voyage was the restoration of Bro. Ross Taylor's little boy Artie, from brain-fever, without the use of medicines. Miss Dr. Meyers and Dr. Johnson of the party, and the ship's surgeon, pronounced the child critically ill, and summed up its case in the expression: "one chance in two for life even on land." The mother and father believing in healing of the body of sickness in answer to prayer of faith, hesitated as to what course to pursue. They went with earnest prayer, and said they felt assured that there should no medicines be used. The ship's surgeon and purser sent for Brother Taylor, and told him he must have the child regularly treated; if not, and it died, then he would have him arrested in England for murder. To this Brother Taylor replied, he had not been accustomed to having anyone interfere with his family, and he did not propose to have. He preferred trusting God, rather than physicians and medicines.

The next day he took the child ·in his arms on deck, and showed it to the ship's physician. He said, " He looks all right now." On the very day the child was so ill and the doctors had pronounced its case very doubtful, I saw the child sit at the dinner table on his father's lap, and drink soup out of a spoon.

Now as to the weather, etc. We encountered a severe storm. On Tuesday, the 27th, it began, and continued until Wednesday night, the wind blowing a gale behind us, drove the high waves after us, and the only hope was to get away from them by running the ship at her best. This was done, until the engineer reported to the captain that the wheel was so often out of water, that its revolutions in air became so violent, and on being plunged into the water again was so suddenly checked, that his machinery was in danger of breaking. The captain then gave instructions to stop or slow down, which being done, the seas overtook us. One coming over us in such weight and with such force as to break through the companion-way and flood the saloon and state-rooms below to considerable depth, — calling us out of our state-rooms to anticipate the very near appearance of death. We formed a line — those who were fortunate to be well enough — and handed water from one man to another, and emptying it into the scuppers of the ship until, in about one hour and a half, we had the water reduced, and, in the meantime, the danger being communicated to the captain, the sailors came and mended the break with canvas, so that it would shed the greater part of the

seas, which now only occasionally broke over us.
The captain, having seen the two dangers, chose
what he considered the least, and ordered a full
head of steam, which, when put on, kept us out
of the danger of foundering which was threaten-
ing. There was consternation among some of
the crew, but our party were all calm, and
worked and prayed; though at first we thought,
at least some of us, that we were about to be lost,
and receive a watery grave.

The sailors could not understand why it was
that the women were so calm. They did not
scream like women generally do. We explained the reason why women can be calm when
seamen are frightened. We expect to leave
Liverpool to-morrow morning, by the *Biaffra*,
for Loando, the trip extending to about March
21st, on account of the stoppage at various
ports.

I have given you a poor letter, but it is the
best I can do for the very limited time I have.

Your brother,

W. P. Dodson.

The Lord graciously spared the lives of
this company, and we have recorded their
own story. They found many friends in
England, and after a few days' rest, they
sailed away from the shores of Great Britain

for Africa, in the steamer *Biaffra*; but Brother M'Kinley was too sick to sail either to Africa or to America. The peace of God possessed his soul, and he sweetly resigned himself to the will of God, though, no doubt, it was one of the greatest crosses of his life.

If ever his satanic majesty hated a company of saints, it seems to me he hated these missionaries, and if it had been in his province as "the prince of the power of the air" to have drowned them in the deepest sea, I have no doubt he would have gladly done so.

Mark the following letter from Levi D. Johnson, M. D. The letter was mailed at Madeira Island, February 12, where the steamer *Biaffra* stopped on which they sailed from Liverpool to Africa. He says:—

"I had a blessed experience one terrible stormy night. Would that I could paint it as I saw it. Had suffered much all day, and was weary with the tossing of the ship. During the night I dreamed I was here under just my present circumstances. I thought a storm was raging on the deep and I trying to keep in my bunk. I arose and looked out over the waste of

troubled waters and saw the Angel of Death
flying directly toward the ship. I at once recog-
nized him and in a few moments he entered my
state-room and stood in front of me, and looking
me squarely in the face said, 'Who are you?'
I replied, 'I am a poor worm of the dust, *washed
in the blood of Jesus*. My name is Levi D.
Johnson and I am now on my way from America to Africa to carry the good news of the
gospel of Jesus Christ to dark benighted hearts.'
For an instant he looked at me intensely, then
said as he hastened away, 'I could not drown
you if I would.' Instantly I awoke and a calm
sense of absolute safety filled my whole being.
How good our Father is to give us these man-
ifestations of His love and pity. Bless His
name. I do love Him. . . ."

Rev. A. E. Withey, one of Bishop Taylor's
missionaries, writes from Funchall, Madeira
Islands, February 12:—"Here we are ashore in
this Paradise of the Lord. It seems like a
dream to be here. We were met by the agent
of the British and Foreign Bible Society, who
shows us much kindness. The Bishop told him
to watch for us. We shall overtake the *Nubia*
at Cape Bonney and expect to meet Bishop
Taylor there. All are in good spirits and happy.
All are well except Sister Willis and she is
improving. Glory be to God! Our next stop-

ping place is Sierra Leone. We will not reach
Loando until March 22nd, making over thirty
stops. We go up the Congo twelve miles to
Banana, the outpost of the Congo missions. We
have an offer from a trader on the Congo to
support two men a year, give land for school,
and lend fifty negroes a day to help build.
Well, bless the Lord we are following the dear
Holy Spirit and He is such a Comforter. Our
danger is in forgetting Him. As long as we
keep filled with the Holy Spipit all goes well.
O! love Divine, how sweet Thou art! Glory to
God! This is a wonderful gathering together
of workers from all points of the compass.
There are stalwart characters here, who will be
heard from if we keep our leader the Holy
Ghost. Love to all."

Dr. Johnson wrote the following letter
from Port Funchal, Madeira, February 11th,
as follows :—

The first days out from Liverpool to this
place were very stormy. The ocean was not so
rough as on the passage from New York to
England, but more of a clopped sea. We
skirted the Bay of Biscay for two and a half
days. This is always noted for roughness.
The past few days have been pleasant, and the
sea smooth, with the exception of heavy, dead

swells. We are now lying at sea, six or seven miles from the Island of Madeira; will go into port in the morning. We take on coal, water and provisions here; will stop five or six hours. We will not make another call until we reach Sierra Leone, W. C. Africa, a sail of eleven or twelve days if everything is prosperous. From there our journey will be slow and tedious, stopping at all the coast towns. It will take us from forty to forty-five days from here to reach Loando.

FEB. 12.—At anchor. The grandest sight I ever saw in natural scenery. The island is of volcanic formation. Mountains rise 5,000 to 5,856 feet. Mountain sides very green, and the houses all *white*, which give the island a beautiful appearance.

The remembrance of our dear Friends in America is very precious. It is a comfort, which I hardly think you can fully appreciate, to know that you are continually holding us up before a throne of grace with strong prayers and crying before God.— *Gospel Expositor*.

This happy band of faithful workers arrived safe at their journey's end and the American Consul telegraphed the fact to the Secretary of State of this country, and it was published in the *Boston Herald*.

So far the providence of God has smiled upon this great enterprise, and so He will continue to do.

One of the Missionaries in this band sends the following, which I take from the *Christian Standard:*—

STEAMSHIP BIAFFRA, OFF SENEGAMBIA, 170 MILES.

WEDNESDAY, Feb. 18th, 1885.

" We are now facing almost east, and making our way, under that great shed of country, bounded by Senegambia and Guinea; and are soon to land at Sierra Leone, and thence go to Cape Palmas. We expect to take the Bishop on board at Bonney, in about two weeks. It is most beautiful summer. We are occupying the after deck of the ship, with an awning over us, and bananas hanging above our heads; people sitting around in willow chairs, reading, talking, writing, or gazing off at sea, or sky; for there is no land to look at, and no sign of ship, or vessel, except at long intervals. This 'life on the ocean wave,' in the South Atlantic, with precious religious meetings three times a day, and all bodily comforts attended to, furnishes a contrast with the ' perils and privations,' which at the start, we learned, might be expected. Once in a while, I look ahead, but all in perfect trust. I look home-ward, but not as ' Lot's wife.' We will be in

Sierra Leone to-morrow; I suppose we will not be allowed to go ashore. A party of Baptist missionaries did so, some months ago, and some of the party died soon after. They disregarded proper precautions. I am sorry we are not to stop at Monrovia. I could spend all my time in writing and reading, but there is work, even here on the ship, which is a preparation for the experiences ahead; and to this I must devote myself. In my next I will try to tell you of our party, from whom I receive nothing but love and kindness.

THURSDAY MORNING, Feb. 19.

I have just come on deck, after a refreshing bath of sea water under the hose; and am seated at the side of the ship, beholding for the first time, African land. We are at Freetown, Sierra Leone, fast coming into harbor. The sun is just appearing over the port. To the right, hills arise, which grow into mountains, beginning in amber and ending in blue. I can see the foliage, which we wonder at as we go through botanical gardens at home. Some of the specimens overtop the rest, and look like giraffe sentinels looking out to sea. I have just caught sight of the first native, in a canoe, fishing; black, how black! almost naked. They say they can equal Satan quoting scripture; can sing psalms and hymns; but are the biggest thieves along the coast.

The captain stopped one this morning going down the companion-way, with one of the large willow chairs. The port holes are all kept closed while here. What lovely scenes appear while we look through the glasses. I would like to go ashore, but our party feels God has not called us here, and the Bishop has warned us of the risk of health, so we do not want to tempt God. Wonderful are the sights I have seen, and what scenes are before me ; but day by day, with sweet surprise my heart is prepared. I love God more, I love my country, I love my loved ones at home, more and more as I love God's kingdom, and seek it first. This is God's plan, I've been told often, but never so learned it before."   WM. P. DODSON.

(The following dispatch will be read with devout thankfulness, by all who watch with prayerful interest the advance of Bishop Taylor and his missionaries into benighted Africa.—ED.)

"The United States Consul at Sierra Leone, under date of February 25, reports to the Department of State the arrival there of Dr. William Taylor, the American Bishop for Africa."—*Peninsula Methodist.*

" William Taylor is in Africa. Good and great men have gone to the ' dark continent.'

But it is safe to say *no man* ever went to Africa watched with deeper interest, loved more intensely by holy people, more believed in by Christians generally and followed with more prayers of faith than William Taylor. Is there another man in Christendom who could find forty men and women in six months to go with him on the terms laid down in Matthew, tenth chapter? We believe not one. God bless William Taylor is the prayer, perhaps, of one million devout Christians of various denominations in America. Yea, Australia, South Africa, India, the West Indies and Europe find thousands more doing so. January 27th was Brother Taylor's date for Liberia. After settling everything there he is to meet his heroic band at Loando, west coast of Africa, from which they strike for the interior."—*India Methodist Watchman.*

The blessing of God still attends this glorious missionary work. Mark the goodness of God in the following letter from Bishop Taylor:—

BONNEY, EAST GUINEA, AFRICA, Feb. 26th, 1885.

Dear Brother Grant,—I think I wrote you that after the session of the Liberia Conference

I spent a Sabbath at Virginia, seventeen miles up the St. Paul's River, from Monrovia, and preached Monday night at Muhlenburg, the Lutheran Mission, Rev. Mr. Day. On Tuesday night I preached again in Monrovia and baptized sixteen of our new converts — over fifty were converted to God during our series at Monrovia. On Saturday, the 14th inst., I took passage South on the S. S. *Nubia*. That was the ship on which our people were to sail from Liverpool, February 4, but instead, the *Nubia* sailed from Liverpool on the 25th of January, and the steamship *Biaffra* sailed with our people February 4. I learned of this change, which was in our favor in ship accommodation, when I went aboard the *Nubia*.

Sunday morning early we anchored off Grand Bassa, eighty miles south of Monrovia, and remained there till Monday evening. On that Sabbath I preached three times, had an ordination of a Deacon in the morning and an Elder in the evening, and administered the sacrament of the Lord's supper.

On Tuesday morning we anchored off Sinoe, one hundred and sixty miles south of Monrovia. During the four hours the ship lay at anchor, though it took nearly an hour to pull to the shore and the same time for returning, I preached in our Church ashore, administered baptism, and ordained a Deacon.

On Wednesday evening I left the *Nubia* at Cape Palmas, two hundred and forty miles from Monrovia. I preached in our Church there Wednesday night.

On Thursday, at 10.30 A. M., I preached again and ordained two Deacons. All these had been elected to orders at previous sessions of the Conference, but could not attend the recent session. I preached again Thursday night. On Friday noon I preached at Tubmantown, four miles inland, to a full house. I preached again at our Church in Cape Palmas on Friday night, and twelve seekers came forward for prayers. On Saturday I visited two native towns in the neighborhood, and preached at night in our Church; sixteen seekers forward and nine saved. These all took it in the old way — awful screaming and crying for pardon, and when saved shouted all over the house, and all through the streets as they went home. Next day, Sabbath 22d, the *Biaffra* was due at Cape Palmas, but we hoped that she would not come till Monday, and we hoped to get a large number more saved. I went to a love feast at 6.30 A. M., but in half an hour a messenger came and announced the arrival of our ship — sharp on time. I hastened to my quarters at the house of Rev. C. H. Harmon, our Presiding Elder for Cape Palmas District, and he had his boat and Kroomen ready, and we pulled off — Bro. Harmon, Capt. Yeates (of

Yeates, Porterfield & Co., Wall street, New York) and many of our brethren accompanied me to the ship. I had not heard anything concerning my dear missionaries since I sailed from New York on the 13th of December, except the note from you saying that Ross and family had telegraphed that they would be on hand — which I had given up as a hopeless case, and hence knew not whether I should see my dear Ross and family or not. So as we pulled out the first mate of the *Biaffra* hailed me and I said, " Is my son on board?" "Yes, he and his family." "Are all my missionaries alive and well?" "Yes." I bowed my head and wept, and thanked God. So I soon went up the ship's ladder and had a joyful meeting with my fellow-laborers. Archdeacon Hamilton, Church Missionary Society, by regular order, took the morning service. I preached to the Kroomen on the deck at 3 P. M., and preached to my people and the other passengers at 8 P. M.

We are all getting on nicely except Miss Reese, the Quakeress from Indiana. She was remarkably well on the *City of Montreal*, but the tropics has revived an old complaint of hers, which she hoped had been fully cured, and now she is very ill — not African fever at all, but an old complaint revived by a change of climate or from some other cause. She is a grand young lady, and will do well in Africa, if the Lord will, or better in heaven.

Brother Clarence L. Davenport, and Miss Mary R. Myers, M. D., were married aboard the *Biaffra*, yesterday, at 3 P. M. I performed the ceremony, assisted by Archdeacon Hamilton. The captain, officers and all hands made a great occasion — cannon fired every ten minutes for an hour, presents given, etc.

No room or time to speak of accounts, which Bro. Withey will explain to you. We were induced from representations in England, to buy more than we had designed. The Lord has given the funds what you have and what I have to square all — but I will need all I have, so the Lord will help you to pay Fowler Bros. No time to read this over — mail going. I am perfectly well.

WILLIAM TAYLOR.

CHAPTER VIII.

ESTABLISHING MISSIONS IN CENTRAL AFRICA.

" Though now the nations.sit beneath
The darkness of over-spreading death,
God will arise with light divine,
On Zion's holy towers to shine."

" That light shall shine on distant lands,
And wandering tribes in joyful bands,
Shall come, thy glory, Lord, to see,
And in thy courts to worship thee."

SURELY, " All the ends of the earth shall
see the salvation of God." He " that sitteth
between the cherubims will shine forth," and
" the glory of the Lord shall cover the earth
as the waters cover the sea." It was in the
faith that such promises inspire that Bishop
Taylor and his band started to evangelize
the wandering tribes of Africa. No wonder
that many good people were full of doubts
about this African expedition. It was only
the eye of faith that could see the invisible;

and the heart of faith that could repose upon Him, that dared to leave home and plunge into the interior of a wild, heathen country and undertake to bring order out of moral confusion, and beauty out of such moral deformity. But, all things are possible to him that believeth, and all things are possible with God. In the spirit of these two possibilities, Bishop Taylor and his noble band of men, women and children landed at Loando, March 19, 1885 ;— *Strangers in a hostile land.*

Loando is the capital of the Portuguese province of Angola. It has 11,000 inhabitants, one-third of them are Europeans, most of whom have been sent out as convicts.

In the providence of God, Dr. Summers had engaged a large mansion in this city containing twenty rooms and spacious grounds, located on an elevated and lovely spot, and swept by the daily sea breezes. This estate cost $15,000, but was bought for $8,000 by the generosity of an American philanthropist. For a time they paid $50.00 a month for rent. Flour cost $20.00 per barrel; fresh water had to be carried ten miles, and cost $1.00 per day, and all this, and much more, must

be bought with cash.   But the above philanthropist had given Bishop Taylor $1,000 for
this emergency.

At this missionary headquarters, this party
had to wait, (1) because the king of Angola
was away from home, and the Bishop would
not go forth without the moral support of the
king's personal approval, (2) they had to
wait to learn the language, and especially to
get acclimated.   At different times, each of
them had the African fever, except the
Bishop and Mrs. Mead, who had six children
to care for, and had no time to take the
fever.   The Bishop says he is put up to keep
in all climates.

Charles Miller, of Baltimore, was one of
the finest young men of the whole company,
who had an excellent and well preserved
body, and a well cultivated mind, and a
warm, zealous heart, and promised to do
excellent service for God; but, when he was
stricken with fever, he firmly resolved that
he would take Christ for his Healer, and
would take no kind of medicine.   He claimed
that God would satisfy him with long life
and show him his salvation.   So when he
was sick, he wrote in his diary, "Healed of

diarrhœa; resisted in faith the fever," and again, "In faith against the fever. A steady faith wins. I am delivered from African fever." Meanwhile the fever was taking his precious life. Bishop Taylor and others urged him to take quinine, and break up the fever, as others had done, but he refused till it was too late; for when he cried for the doctor and medicine, and the fever yielded to treatment, his body was too far gone to rally. As the Bishop stood by him, and his face was beaming with a winning smile, he said, "Bishop, that is delightful;" at another time he sang out, "Ship a-hoy!" His work was done; he died in peace, and entered into eternal rest.

Mark well the following just conclusions of Bishop Taylor on this topic:—

"The faith by which dear Charlie became a child of God, and was sanctified wholly, rested on the immutable Word of God; but his insurance policy, guaranteeing long life in Africa by a continuous miracle, without any medical means, lacked such an immutable basis, and was therefore presumption, and not faith. He had, indeed, as we since learned, accepted as infallible—as the Word of God—the extreme views of certain

good men who claim to be expositors of faith
healing, entirely ignoring all healing remedies or
arts.   They affirm that ' many are now beginning
to see that the body is inseparably connected with
the spirit and soul in God's thought of full salvation.'   If we allow the time that God has set
for the completion of this work for our bodies —
the resurrection day — all right.   But these ex-
tremists claim to have found in the Holy Scriptures a basis of faith available to all believers,
on which it is their privilege and duty to receive
Christ as a Physician for their bodies, to preserve
them from attacks of disease ; or if attacked by
any form of disease or injury, to be suddenly
healed in answer to prayer alone ; and that this
perfect healing of the body is a concomitant of
a perfect healing of the soul by faith, and rests
on a foundation of Divine revelation of equal
authority and availability as the believing soul's
basis of faith in the record of God concerning
His Son.   If these two things are ' inseparably
connected,' and this two-fold basis of faith is
alike reliable for a present ' full salvation ' for
the body as well as the soul, then they stand or
fall together ; and every believer's spiritual
attainments must be limited and gauged by his
condition of bodily health, or want of health.
This teaching has no more identity with holiness,

nor with Scriptural faith healing, than a parasite has with the oak on which it foists itself."

We may take a look at Loando, and into the interior of that missionary mansion by reading the following letter :—

" Rev. Clarence Davenport writes to his mother as follows from Loanda, April 2d :

'We have been so busy and burdened with work, that until we systematized things we had scarcely time to breathe. The result was that on the 29th of March, I was prostrated with the African fever, and on the 30th, Mary took it. We were both very sick and consequently are very weak. And having been obliged to sleep in the room where are our daily headquarters, we have had but little chance to recuperate. Our minds have been overtaxed as well as our bodies. While lying prostrate with the fever, one of the brethren brought us letters from home. The sight of letters made us feel better.

April 7th.—We obtained possession of the upper part of the house, have two cosy little rooms, and now we have a little time, our own, under God. I am glad also to report almost complete health, as far as wife and I are concerned ; but sorry to report seven of our number sick with the fever, but none seriously. The houses of the whites in Loando are built of mud

and stone, tile roofs, walls eighteen inches thick,
and two stories high. Native houses are built of
bamboo, with thatched roof. The native part of
the village is laid out as beautifully as that of the
whites. The soil is exceedingly rich, and productive. I have been doing the marketing for
the last few days, and do not have any trouble in
making myself understood. I use a little talk
and considerable pantomime. The latter when
backed by the money accomplishes wonders.
Wife and I feel finely to-day, in both body and
soul. We find here a large field for the exercise
of all the patience we can get. But we also find
Jesus abundantly able to supply all our needs,
and we are beholding Him in all His beauty, and
are constrained to magnify and bless His holy
name. Since we landed we have been very busy.
Most of our company are very busy learning
Portuguese."

On their way down the coast Bishop
Taylor decided to establish one mission at
Mayumba, because one of the traders promised to sustain a man and wife for one year.
Rev. H. W. Willis and wife, B. F. Northam
and Carl Steelman were appointed there.
After a variety of experiences, and a long
sickness on the part of Mrs. Willis, she
returned to America and her husband took

the fever at old Calaba on the coast of Africa, and died on his way, and sleeps in the mighty deep with Dr. Coke and many others. Mrs. Willis reached this country, and has been made a blessing to many since her return.

This mission was finally established at Mamba, in a region that is thickly dotted with small towns, and not far from Mayumba; and is under the care of B. F. Northam, and assisted by Henry E. Benoit of Canada. They have built a house and are doing good among the people.

Brother Withey and family were quite sick for a time, but God delivered them all, he writes:

"I was made to triumph in the heat of the figry trial and rejoiced. How Jesus revealed Himself to me and I had real joy. "Count it all joy," Well, I have seen no trace of desire on the part of any member of my family to 'look back,' but rather we are "strong in the Lord and *in the power of His might.*"

For various reasons this missionary band were delayed in Loando for two months. Meanwhile, Dr. Summers had explored the interior to Malange, and returned. The Bishop writes as follows:

On the 29th of May, with a small pioneer party of my men, I took Steamer for Dondo, leaving all our women and children, and a few men, in our very comfortable quarters at Loando. I thought it best that a small party should go first and select suitable sites for Mission stations, and provide houses for our families. Most of our people were down with fever, so that but few could travel; and some who were able for the journey had to remain to take care of the sick and look after the stuff.

Our first selection was in Nhanguepepo, 51 miles, by a foot-path, from Dondo. On the 19th of June I wrote our people in Loando to come on to the interior immediately, to occupy Nhanguepepo, Pungo Andongo, and Malange, giving in my letter the appointment of each, his field of labor according. as I believe, with the will of God.

Waiting till the middle of July, and hearing nothing from my people in Loando, I and Murray McLean, and 16 carricadors, went to Dondo, hoping to meet all or a part of them on their arrival at the place; but we could get no information in regard to them. After waiting in Dondo three days, a letter came saying that 120 cargoes (manloads), with Samuel J. Mead, wife, and niece, and Bros. Levin Johnson and C. W. Gordon, had left Loando by steamer the 15th of

June. With the ordinary body of water in the Coanza River, they would have reached Dondo (240) miles in four days; but after two years of drought, the water was so low that it took 14 days for the party to get through. We had experienced so much trouble and extra cost in securing carricadors, that I gave up all hope of help from the merchants and traders, who said they could not get men to carry their merchandise; but I got access to God, and a blessed assurance, that with a little care to give information of our need to the villagers of Nhanguepepo, we should have them come to us in sufficient numbers for all our purpose; and so it turned out.

Bro. Samuel Mead and Arda his wife, and Bros. Johnson and Gordon, had long been ill, especially the young men; but they all arrived in good health, and full fleshed. They were all appointed to Malange, and the two young men, in charge of a large proportion of their cargoes, pushed directly on to their destination; but the Meads remained in Nhanguepepo till the larger party arrived from Loando. I received a letter, meantime, stating that they would leave Loando Aug. 6, and be due in Dondo the 21st. So, on the 20th, Bro. McLean and I, and a force of carriers, arrived from Nhanguepepo, and found that, instead of 14 days, they had come through in 10 days, hence had been waiting for us 4 days.

Dondo is the largest town in Angola, except Loando. It is the head of steamboat navigation, and the termination of the great caravan routes from the far interior; but its deadly climate had precluded it from our list of fields to be occupied at once. On my last preceding visit there, however, the *chefe* of Dondo and a few other leading citizens waited on me, with a request that I should establish a Mission in Dondo. So now the question was pending whether it might not be the will of God that Rev. C. L. Davenport, Mary Davenport, M. D., and C. M. McLean, whom we had thought to station in the Kioko country, should not for the present stop and found a Mission in Dondo. This last party from Loanda consisted of Rev. Amos Edwin Withey, wife, and four children; Mrs. Minnie Mead and six children (Wm. H. Mead, her husband, being one of our pioneer party at Nhanguepepo); Mrs. Wilks and daughter Agnes (Bro. Wilks having been settled in Pungo Andongo); also, Bro. and Sister Davenport. It was arranged that Bro. McLean should conduct all the party, with half their cargoes, to Nhanguepepo, while I and the Davenports should remain in Dondo till Bro. McLean should return with the carriers for the remaining cargo. Meantime we would find out the will of God concerning the immediate occupaion of Dondo.

Some persons in that rough country travel on the backs of bulls; but the most respectable way of traveling there is in a topoiya—a covered frame-work suspended from a bamboo pole, and carried by two men. The orthodox number for a traveler is six men, who alternate at the pole, and also carry his luggage. Carricadors carry cargoes only, and topoiya men claim their business to be quite distinct from the other, and more honorable. Our men, like myself, took it afoot; but our ladies and the children were hardly equal to that, on as quick time as we were in the habit of making. We got the cargoes distributed among the carricadors on hand, without much trouble; but the topoiya men all wanted to carry the children, but not their mothers—especially Sister Wilks, who declined to give her weight, but admitted that it was at least 180 lbs., a formidable load for two men, over rugged mountains and deep gulches. Much time and persuasion were required to get men to agree to carry the 'mulher grande;' but finally it was arranged. On the morning for departure I took nine of the children afoot to Pambos, distant a four-mile climb up the hills, there to await the arrival of the party. We waited long, and finally all came on except Sister Mead and Sister Wilks. Their topoiya men, under some sort of a dodge, had "skipped out," and came up to Pambos without any load. So we had to have a " big palaver," and I engaged six of the men to return with me and bring on the two ladies. On our return to Dondo, we found that Sister Wilks had been stricken down with an attack of African fever, so Sister Mead went on and Sister Wilks remained under treatment of Sister Davenport. During the week of detention till Brother McLean could return with the carriers, Sister Wilks fully recovered, and Brother and Sister Davenport and all concerned saw unmistakably that the Lord had called them to build in Dondo,— 1. To open a day school in the town ; 2. An industrial department, under Brother McLean, a little way out; and 3. If a boarding school should be required, to build on a mountain near, high and healthy ; and by anticipation we laid out 250 acres of land, including the mountain, and petitioned the Governor-General for the grant of it. In that week of work and Divine illumination, it became apparent to me that I ought to sail for Lisbon, October 15 ; visit London and Liverpool and return."

Till that time the Bishop went on planting his missions, and organizing churches, and examining his candidates for local preachers, and holding a District Conference at Nhanguepepo, and procuring houses for his men, and

VILLAGE ON THE WEST COAST OF AFRICA. A PALAVER TREE.

laying out 2,500 acres of land for an industrial farm at Nhanguepepo, and procuring cattle for his farm, and, indeed, making every possible preparation.

The Bishop writes, August 26 :—

"We have twelve children, ranging from sixteen years to two, all except the two younger will be helpers in missionary work from the start —real helpers in Christian life and influence, and in learning and teaching the language. Our twelve children are a grand missionary investment."

The Bishop was as jubilant as a bird in spring, singing his song of triumph.

"Though troubles assail, and dangers affright,
Though friends should all fail, and foes all unite,
Yet one thing secures us, whatever betide,
The promise assures us, ' The Lord will provide.'

The birds, without barn or store-house, are fed;
From them let us learn to trust for our bread;
His saints what is fitting shall ne'er be denied,
So long as 'tis written, ' The Lord will provide.'

When Satan appears to stop up our path,
And fills us with fears, we triumph by faith;
He cannot take from us, though oft he has tried,
The heart-cheering promise,'The Lord will provide.' ''

Mrs. Dr. Davenport was made very useful

in her profession during the sickness of her associates. She and her husband were quite sick, but they regained their health, and were eager to enter the interior. She writes to her mother, July 24 :—

" We have so far no fault to find with Africa. The Lord is taking care of us. It is remarkable that a company as large we were should have suffered so little on theWest coast of Africa. The traders who came on the Biafra with us and stopped at different points above us, prophesied and told us that it was folly for us to come to Africa, that we would all die, etc., and as for bringing women and children here and expecting them to live, that was simply absurd. We have heard from a reliable source that two of them died, and also a clerk of one of the traders, while two or three are going home for their health, cannot stay, and some of the others have fared worse than we in regard to sickness."

Mrs. Davenport writes of her husband, when he started for the interior on foot :—

" Clarence wore a blue flannel suit, over his thick, strong overalls. On his head a helmet, which I had covered with white cotton cloth to keep out rays of heat. In his knapsack on his back, he had two or three books, money, and many little things. In his haversack on one side he carried two loaves of bread, a can of salmon, some gingerbread, knife and fork and drinking cup."

Mr. Davenport writes, September 1 :—

" July 29, at 4.30 P. M., Immanuel and I bade our friends and my beloved wife farewell and set our faces toward the interior, accompanied by a man to carry our blankets. At 4.35 we passed out of the town, and taking a foot-path, went single file. When we had lost sight of Loando I knelt down and asked Jesus to help us. I found Immanuel kneeling beside me with uncovered head. We marched on until after eight, part of the time by starlight; sometimes through grass higher than my head. We then stopped at an encampment of carriers. It was quite a sight. Some were lying huddled around a camp fire. After resting three-fourths of an hour, we started onward and marched an hour and a half, when Immanuel became so sleepy that I ordered a halt and we spread our beds; the two colored men slept an hour and a quarter, while I fought mosquitos and thought. At the end of that time we again took up our line of march, and shortly after 2, reached another encampment of carriers. Here we found a large party going our way, in charge of Lieut.-Col. Veitor, military commander of the province.

About 3 we again marched on, and did not stop till daylight. We had moonlight from 9 till 3. The scenery by moonlight was enchanting. About 9 A. M. we reached Calumba, still 12 miles from the place where I expected to catch the steamer from Dondo."

Mr. Davenport, having reached Dondo, with the rest of the party, he wrote :—

"Last Tuesday, the Bishop, Mary and I explored a high mountain, about two miles from Dondo, which has an elevation of about 1,500 feet. We were much pleased with our exploration. That night I had a short but severe attack of fever, but was all right by next night.

On Saturday the Bishop, Brother McLean and I stepped off the amount of land we wanted, about 522 acres, including the mountain.

We have decided to remain in Dondo, for a time at least. On Saturday Mary was taken sick with a fever, and grew worse till last night when her tongue became thick, speech difficult, delirium imminent. Having done all we could, we looked to God, and He answered our prayers.

September 2. Mary has a little fever to-day, but not much ; so you see what sort of an introduction we have had to our field of labor. Yet to-day we feel that we are in the order of God, and have stronger faith in Him than ever before. The Bishop left Monday for Nhanguepepo, to hold a district conference as he goes through. Sister Wilks goes on to Pungo Andongo, thirty-seven miles from N., where her husband is stationed.

The Bishop will be back here by the last of the month, on his way back to Loando, thence to England and Portugal, where he spends a few weeks ere returning to Liberia, to hold the next Annual Conference in January. He expects to labor in Liberia till May, when he expects another company of missionaries, whom he will lead to their fields of labor as he has done with us.

Brother W. P. Dodson writes :—

"The trip down the coast from Loando to the mouth of the Coanza, and up the river, a total distance of 240 miles, was a wonderful one. When it was first talked of in America, I thought of it as a ride in perhaps a little scow or tug, and living on hard crusts, or something of the kind ; but it proved very different ; in fact, it was equal to any Hudson river trip, not only in point of scenery (though of vastly different style), but the accommodations were surprising, and far surpassed either ocean steamers, the "Montreal" or the "Biafra." The boat, the "Serpo Pinto," is so built, that while broad and long, she can carry an extensive and heavy burden, and only draw three or four feet of water."

With many disappointments, difficulties
and long journeys, the Bishop succeeded in
locating his workers at the various stations.
He traveled, himself, 600 miles. When he
returned from Malange to Nhanguepepo, he
held a district conference. The conference
elected A. E. Withey, W. P. Dodson and
Charles G. Rudolph a publishing committee,
for a small monthly paper and some primary
school books ; also made two local preachers
and recommended four candidates for admis-
sion into the Liberia conference.

PRESIDING ELDER'S DISTRICT.

After spending a night with God in prayer
the Bishop made out the following appointments in Central Africa, with Rev. A. E.
Withey, Presiding Elder.

EQUATORIAL.

I. *Mamba*, a purely native town, inland
from Mayumba, two degrees South of the
Equator. F. B. Northam was alone after Brother Willis and wife left, till Henry E. Benoit,
of Canada, arrived, who had been associated
with the Salvation Army. He went out in
October, to teach and preach in the French
language. He will be all the more useful as

Mamba belongs to a French Colony. Thus God carries on his work.

II. *St. Paul De Loando*, the port of entry for Angola. Chas. A. Ratcliffe and Ela Chatelain are there teaching English, and French, and learning the Portuguese and the Umbunda languages.

III. *Dondo*, C. L. Davenport, Chas. Murray McLean, Mrs. Mary Davenport, M. D., are stationed there. They have started two self-supporting schools and are learning the language so that they can preach the gospel.

IV. *Nhanguepepo*, fifty-one miles from Dondo, over the highway of the caravans, through the rugged mountainous country. The Bishop writes of this place :

" There, by the generosity of a dear friend in London, we have bought houses for the residence of a working force at present, and a receiving station for yearly recruits, where they can get their seasoning and learn languages to fit them for their work further inland. We have stationed at Nhanguepepo two men with their wives, and two single men—each one has a special department of work assigned him—a press, and a printer to run it ; an industrial school farm, and a man to manage it; a school for ten of our missionary children, besides a native school—all earnest Christians, and will make good missionaries as soon as they can master the languages that will give them access to the heads and hearts of the people."

A. E. Withey Presiding Elder, Wm. H. Mead, Wm. P. Dodson, Chas. D. Rudolph, Mrs. A. Withey, Mrs. W. H. Mead, Miss Nellie Mead, and ten children are located here.

This populous station is twenty-five hundred feet higher than Loando, and is surrounded with mountains on every side. The Governor has given them here twenty-five hundred acres of land, in a beautifully fertile spot, which lies in rolling hills and fruitful valleys. The Coanza river runs by it, only a mile away. No wild beasts have been found here, but deers, hares, rabbits, monkeys, a large goose like bird, and partridges have been found.

Here is the casava root, which is a splendid boiling vegatable, and is dried and made into flour, farina, tapioca, and starch. Bananas, oranges, limes, pine-apples and custard-apples abound, you can buy a large hen for fifteen cents, a goat giving milk, for $1.50, a milch cow for $10.00, and two eggs for a cent. Beans, corn, sweet potatoes, yams and peanuts are plenty.

Brother Mead is starting a farm, and soon expects a pair of oxen to use with the American yoke and plough. So things are settling down to regular work.

Brother Dodson has opened a school under a tent and is teaching. He writes as follows:

"I have already raised a native school. At 8 o'clock in the morning, if here, you would notice the little children in a long line making their way across the hills to school. Their school-house at present consists of a tent-fly caught at one end to a stone wall surrounding the house of the Commandant of this district, the other end supported by a pole and staked on either side to the ground. Under this, I have taught for five days in the week since Monday, June 26th. My desk is my lap as I sit on a sawed off stool, with the children on mats, spread on the ground. Sometimes they get there before I do, and run out to meet me, singing "Happy Day" (their latest accomplishment), clinging about me, and in many ways showing themselves grateful for what they learn. They are taught by the phonetic system, with which I familiarized myself during the voyage here in connection with object teaching.

This will suffice to assure friends that 'the lines are fallen to me in pleasant places,' that I have been shielded from dangers and kept from possible death which were so frequently sounded in my ears, as likely to befall me. In this way I can reach friends to whom I have not opportunity now to write, and in this way also invite messages from them; the distance is great, but my mail matter, letters and papers, come safely."

It was at this station that Bishop Taylor proposed to Brother Dodson to dig a well, so that fresh water would not have to be carried a mile from the river, or from distant hills. They found a favorable spot and the Bishop dug through the first layer of soil, and then lay down, while Brother Dodson dug the second; at a depth of six feet they found water. Amid great joy they resolved to deepen the well.

Brother Dodson says:

"As I lay on the grass, looking at the man of God, who had received honors at the hands of the world, 'esteeming the reproach of Christ greater riches than the treasures of' any spiritual Egypt. dirty from head to foot, dressed in a pair of overalls and a thin shirt, I thought of what infinitely *small* importance is the question 'Is William Taylor a Bishop?' compared with the valuation of such a man in the court of heaven.

I enjoyed those days of physical exertion, when we would return to our tent at night and have such precious seasons of communion with God; then to lie down on our cots near together, and talk until overtaken by sleep.

SEPT. 3, 1885.

The first fruits of our farm came in last week in the shape of a pine-apple which grew upon a new plant, and yesterday the first fruits of the self-supporting school came to me in the shape of a hundred pounds of shelled corn, from one of the native gentry. I got down on my knees and prayed, and gave thanks over the provisions and for the fact of God's first indication to us of his pleasure in our mission.

They have seed planted in great variety, with two hundred banana trees, and over four hundred pine-apple plants, large enough for fruit. So this station will be able to feed all the missionaries that go out, as long as they want to stay to learn the language and get acclimated. Thus the Lord opens one door after another for the support and comfort of this mission. Glory to God!

V. *Pungo Andongo.* "From Nhanguepepo we proceed in the same path thirty-seven miles to *Pungo Andongo*, noted for the stupendous cliffs of solid conglomerate of a great variety of small stones, which distinguish the mountain range in which it nestles. It is a town of two or three thousand population. We stationed there a good missionary and his wife, who is his equal in the mission field."

Rev. Joseph W. Wilks and wife and daughter are stationed here, a church and day and Sunday-school have been organized. "Mrs. Wilks is a woman of superior ability in the pulpit, school-room, cornfield or kitchen." So says Bishop Taylor.

VI. *Malange.* "From Pungo Andongo we go on through a woody country-scrub of rounded ridges and valleys, but no high mountains, sixty-two miles to Malange, on the eastern border of the Province of Angola, three hundred and ninety-four miles from Loando. In Malange we stationed four men and two ladies. This is the commencement of a line of stations to be extended (D. V.) year by year to the centre of the continent and onward, as fresh recruits shall arrive.

These are already by Christian example missionary lighthouses."

Samuel J. Mead, W. R. Summers, M. D., Levin Johnson, Chas. W. Gordon, Mrs. Aida Mead, and Miss Bertha Mead were stationed here.

The Bishop says:

"In each place we have an ordained minister

except two, there we have preaching men. A specific department of work is assigned to each man and woman on each station. A. E. Withey is Superintendent of our Angola Mission during my absence. All our people in South Central Africa are settled, and comfortably settled in houses. All were well and hearty, happy and hopeful when I left them, except that L. Johnson and E. Chatelain had occasional relapses."

Continued ill health compelled Levin Johnson at the advice of Dr. Summers, to return to America, where he has regained his health. About the first of September, Brother Davenport opened a night School with seven clerks, and a day School with three children at Dondo. When suddenly turned out of his house, he moved into his tent, but soon found a house, with four rooms and dining-hall, which was secured for five years with the privilege of buying it at any time for three thousand dollars. He made his own furniture, in part, because he could not buy it. He thanks God that he ever learned a number of trades before he left America. "My life in the timber country, work in the tile factory, clerking in the drug store, teaching, carpentering, painting, ministering work, and home training have all tended toward Africa." Bishop Taylor having stationed his workers and made provision for their comfort found that his incessant labor and constant care, and long journeys, had had power to take from him fifty-one pounds of his former self. But he had time to recruit his strength on his journeys to London, Liverpool, Portugal, and Brussels. I am happy to record that the Bishop has as many friends in Europe as in the United States, and they are constantly rendering him material and moral assistance.

BISHOP TAYLOR AT COURT.

December 11, the Bishop writes from London :—

"I have just returned from a trip to Brussels. I went to see Leopold II. in regard to my contemplated expedition up the Congo and the Kasai, into the Tushilange country. It is my custom in going into a new country to plant missions, to make myself and my purpose known at head-quarters."

By official routine it would have taken ten days for the U. S. Minister to secure the Bishop an audience with the King. But

Bishop Taylor had the courage to go straight to the palace, and in thirty minutes he made arrangements for an interview, and in one day he went to see the King without anyone to present him. The King met him at the door, and extending his hand with a hearty welcome, conducted him to a good seat and chatted with him forty minutes. The King is six feet, four, in height, and well proportioned. He was greatly pleased with the prospect of a mission in the Congo State, and would gladly cooperate with all the means in his power. The Bishop also formed an acquaintance with all the heads of the three departments of Government of the Congo State, who have their head-quarters at Brussels. No wonder the Bishop was jubilant, and cried out "Glory to God's holy name forever, Amen!"

About this time, Bishop Taylor issued a tract on self-supporting missions, in which he shows that

" Africa is entirely different as a mission field from both India and South America. In Africa, not of course referring to the British Colonies of the South, we can have no congregations to receive the Gospel through the English language ;

hence we have no appreciable *value* to put into
the market, and cannot on the self-supporting
principle expect something for nothing. In five
of the stations we have opened, we have commenced schools that yeild a support to the
teachers on principle Number 2.

What about those missionaries who are not
engaged in school teaching?

They proceed in their preparatory work under
principle Number 1, which applies to any trade
or profession that a Christian may follow.

" Secularization?"

Yes, of the apostolic sort, secularization sanctified to God, a leverage, to lift perishing people
from the horrible pit of heathenism. In the
schools we have commenced in Angola, we are
providing for an industrial department, so that
our missionaries, under principle Number 1, will
not turn aside to secularities, but make secularities turn aside to them, and every productive
employment at all suited to that country and
necessary to self-support will be embraced in the
industrial school plan and constitute the legitimate work of the teachers so engaged.

Industrial schools are no novelty, but have
been worked with success in old Christian countries, and, to some extent, in heathen lands. In
most of the countries where they have been
introduced they were preceded by all the indus-

tries essential to civilized life, ancient and modern. Industrial schools, therefore, in all such countries are based on a principle of local expediency, but in Africa we found them on the principle of absolute public necessity. Not to speak of the noble missions that slightly fringe the edges of the dark cloud that hangs over the continent, the barbarous millions of Africa live in the main, from hand to mouth, and are hence a migratory people. To educate and Christianize them to an extent at all commensurate with the vast work to be done, we must as quickly as possible settle them. To settle them we must create local attractions and attachments—Christian homes, good farms, good orchards, good houses, good schools, houses of worship, the knowledge of God, and of salvation in Jesus Christ.

The comparatively small amount of money required is cheerfully given by the friends of this movement, who clearly perceive that God is in it, and, without interfering with the missionary societies and their great work, will, under the leading of His Spirit, make it a success."

I have the following testimony from Brother Dodson :—

"One thing I think the Spirit of the Lord tells me, somewhat after the fashion of our Saviour's words of John the Baptist, that of all men living upon the earth to-day, there is none greater than William Taylor. Some may think him great in his forceful handling of the word of God in the sacred desk; others may be impressed by his grand physical appearance and the great work he has accomplished; others may look at his wonderful knowledge of the Scripture, and the plan of redemption, as displayed in his authorship; but I look rather at the childlike simplicity of his life and manner, and his every word; never rebuking but by the 'Thus saith the Lord,' always patient with the impatience, short-comings, and failures of men, which I have seen him endure, as though he was indeed the *servant of all*. His Scripture readings at Loando, at 5.30 A. M., to all who would join him there at that time, I will always recall with wonder and praise. At first, my impressions of his greatness put me at a distance from him, but he said to me one day: 'My brother, you will always find me easy to approach,' and in my frequent walks and talks with him since, I have never lost my deep appreciation for him as a man *wonderfully* endowed of God, though as simple-hearted as a child."

My heart has been greatly blessed in reading the following reflections and spiritual testimony which Bishop Taylor wrote at Loando :

" Back to place of beginning. Our party landed here the 19th of March — a little less, now, than seven months. Oh how much we have lived in seven months ! What a time of sifting, separating, chastening, developing ! God kept us in quarantine for months before He would allow us to advance, and then we walked softly, as in the immediate presence of the King. I have been accustomed to walk with God for forty-four years without a break. Sometimes I have had a special manifestation to my spirit of the Son of God, when it was my pleasure to perceive His distinct personality, and sit in His presence and admire and adore Him, and in melting love sympathize with Him in His stupendous undertaking of bringing our lost race back to God, and feel the wish in my heart — ' O that I could multiply myself into a thousand, and give a thousand years to help Jesus ! ' At other times, a special manifestation of the personal Holy Ghost and the amazing ' love of the Spirit ' for a perishing world, and in adoring love and sympathy put myself entirely at His disposal, to illuminate and lead me according to His own infinite wisdom and love. But ever since I took charge of this expedition to Africa, with no less appreciation and admiration of the personal Jesus and the

personal Holy Sanctifier, I have walked all these
months in the manifestation of the personal presence of God the Father, with such enlarged per-
ceptions of His wisdom, His love, His patience
and forbearance, His infinite desire to adjust the
human conditions essential to the fulfillments of
His covenant pledge to the Redeemer—' to give
Him the heathen for His inheritance, and the
uttermost parts of the earth for his possession,'—I sit in His presence, and more than ever
before weep in adoring love. His special providence over me and my charge, have been continuous and most distinctly discernable. My prayers,
for the most part, are made up of thanksgiving
for His innumerable, immeasurable mercies,
and expressions of undoubting trust for the
timely fulfillment, in detail, of all that He had
engaged to do, and especially that I may see
and do his will, and in no way defeat or mar
any good that God would otherwise bring to pass
as immutable certainty."

From Brussels he wrote to Dr. Carrol of
Baltimore :

"I am in good health. I am abiding in Jesus
and expect to for a million years and on and on
forever. Glory to God! God bless and prosper you !"

Again he writes :

"God has sifted us thoroughly, and for our

good ; and separated from us such as he saw not exactly adapted to our work — though good people — and now His chosen ones are all in their field.

> Knowing what troubles we have seen,
> What conflicts we have past,

I cannot refrain from weeping on every review of the wonderful wisdom and love of God the Father to us, as manifested in the minute details of His special Providence over us. God will make a success of this work worthy of Himself and His methods."

He writes to Rev. Wm. B. Osborn "*I would rather spend my next twenty years with savages in Africa than with the angels in Heaven.*"

Brother Withey writes from Nhanguepepo :

" We wish our friends who are losing sleep on our account, and giving credence to such erroneous reports of our condition as fill the papers that come to us, could spend a week with us, in Nhanguepepo. We are wonderfully located for health, on an eminence overlooking fertile plains, which are surrounded by mountains which one is never tired of looking at. We have cool breezes most of the day, comfortable nights, with very few mosquitoes. A half-hour's walk brings one to the beautiful Coanza River with its scenery. We have a comfortable stone house — the best in the section — have good herds of cattle, good flocks of sheep, goats, and hens. Tenderloin steak for four and a half cents a pound. Pasturage for thousands of cattle. Eggs, six to nine cents a dozen. Corn meal and mandioca flour three and four cents now in time of famine, about one-half cent in time of plenty. Bananas, in their season ten for one cent.

To be sure, we have not had plenty of sugar and butter, but both are 'in the wind.' We are already getting milk from our cows.

We have been bountifully provided for throughout by our Heavenly Father and the Trustees of the Transit Fund, and we are a happy company, who mean to spend our lives in Africa, or anywhere else Jesus Christ may appoint us to, and the sympathy poured upon us by our dear American friends is misplaced. ' Weep not for us,' but for yourselves, if you are not wholly the Lord's and ' walking before Him with a perfect heart ;' but we are exceedingly grateful for the prayers going up for us and for Africa in all parts of the world, and more of these we greatly need, for we are stirred by the lives of Wesley and Fletcher just now, and, beholding the depths of love that they fathomed, we are being

> " Plunged in the Godhead's deepest sea;
> Lost in its immensity."

I have just returned from the Missionary Conference at New York, where the second company of twenty-three missionaries for Africa gave their experience, which thrilled our hearts; they are a heroic band, ready to die or live for God in Africa. They sailed in the City of Chester for Liverpool, March the 20th, 1886; just one year and one day from the time that the first expedition landed at Loando. Surely we are living in marvelous days when whole colonies are going out to enlighten the heathen lands. No doubt some of them go to wear a martyr's crown, and thereby gain a higher seat in glory.

I have just been reading with great interest the travels of Dr. Livingstone through Angola in the years 1854-5.

He says :—

" There is not much knowledge of the Christian religion in either the Congo or Angola, yet it is looked upon with a certain degree of favor. The prevalence of fever is probably the reason why no priest occupies a post in any part of the interior. They come on tours of visitation, and it is said that no expense is incurred, for all the people are ready not only to pay for their services, but also to furnish every article in their power gratuitously. In view of the desolate condition of this fine missionary field, it is more than probable that the presence of a few Protestants would soon provoke the priests, if not to love, to good works."

In the providence of God we have lived to see Bishop Taylor plant four mission stations in the interior of this province of Angola, with more than twenty missionaries who are not afraid of the fever, and who are willing to work with their own hands, and plant their own fields, as far as possible; who, by their Godly lives and triumphant deaths, are spreading the savor of Christ among the people.

The latest news from Bishop Taylor states that he has arranged to found an industrial school, and self-supporting mission at Setta Kroo, on the Liberian coast, and has appointed Wright J. Turner, a promising man of color, to the care of the mission. Mr. Turner has been on the self-supporting plan, among the heathens, all the past year. He expects the Governor will give one thousand acres of land for an industrial farm.

Bishop Taylor writes as follows, February 18, 1886:—

"I want good teachers and missionary apprentices for Liberia, sound Methodists, ready to teach by example in the industrial schools. I do not certainly know, but fear I may not get back by next Conference, but hope to soon after, at any rate. I wish we could push this Liberia work now, but we must plant orchards first in South Central Africa, that our trees of righteousness may be growing.

I am arranging for a preparatory opening of other fields in Liberia besides Setta Kroo immediately, and when we get back, say a year hence, we shall want a hundred missionary workers for Liberia and regions beyond, yearly, till the country is settled with Gospel lighthouses in every direction for a thousand miles. We shall want them in small parties, as many women as men — soul-saving women, good teachers, who can teach the girls plain music, cutting and making clothes, house-work, etc. We can settle a dozen at a time, as fast as they shall come.

We have a big contract. God is leading our friends of the Transit and Building Fund to arrange to do business for him on a scale commensurate with the stupendous work to which God has called us.

Liberia is the garden spot of West Africa — soil, seasons, climate, productions, everything favorable for the best living with the least labor of any country I know of. There are but few farmers here. Nearly all the colonists are traders, and buy their provisions largely from foreign countries. Loaf sugar is twenty-five cents per pound ; butter, one dollar per pound.

Our industrial schools will, under God, work a revolution in this country. Labor is degraded ; hence I work with my hands, as did Paul, as an example for the stuck-up people, and all our missionaries should make up their minds to that as teachers and models for the rising generation. Our people who may come here may expect a little acclimatizing fever, but with the simple treatment we prescribe and a little care, they need have no anxious concern about it. Our people in South Central Africa think no more of an attack of fever than they did of a bad cold at home.

I think Liberia is as healthy as Jersey City any day. I have been here a month, and have seen but two house-flies, and they were on a boat on which I came down St. John's river ; they seemed to be emigrating. I occasionally hear the buzz of a mosquito, but have never seen one. It was just so last year.

Amanda Smith is on this vessel on her first trip to Cape Palmas."

"WILLIAM TAYLOR."

www.ingramcontent.com/pod-product-compliance
Lightning Source LLC
Chambersburg PA
CBHW020811060726
47498CB00017B/2714